CHICKEN FRIEND

Nicola Morgan was born and brought up in a boys' boarding school, where her parents both taught. She studied Classics and Philosophy at Cambridge University, before going on to become a teacher herself and specializing in literacy. But Nicola's ambition was to be an author, and she has now written around seventy home-learning titles, as well as a series of Thomas the Tank Engine stories and several critically acclaimed novels for teens. Her novel *Fleshmarket* won a Scottish Arts Council Award. Nicola lives near Edinburgh, in a house surrounded by woods. *Chicken Friend* is her first book for Walker, and she has more in the pipeline.

Visit: www.nicolamorgan.co.uk

For Bethan, Megan
and Lucy Morgan,
whose families are
absolutely NOT crazy

Chicken Friend

Nicola Morgan

WALKER BOOKS
AND SUBSIDIARIES
LONDON · BOSTON · SYDNEY · AUCKLAND

With thanks to Matilda Webb, for making me believe that chickens have a sense of humour. And to the pupils of Carmuirs Primary School, Falkirk, for their help with the inventions: the robot bin is for you

First published 2005 by Walker Books Ltd
87 Vauxhall Walk, London SE11 5HJ

2 4 6 8 10 9 7 5 3 1

Text © 2005 Nicola Morgan
Cover artwork © 2005 Nick Sharratt

This book has been typeset in Sabon and SoupBone

Printed and bound in Great Britain by Bookmarque Ltd, Croydon, Surrey

British Library Cataloguing in Publication Data:
a catalogue record for this book
is available from the British Library

ISBN 0-7445-9897-4

www.walkerbooks.co.uk

Contents

Stella, Jazz, Mel and My Family

I suppose they're all saying I messed up. Yes, well. I'd like to see you cope any better if you had a family like mine. I was only doing my best. But when you have a family straight out of Crazyville, "best" doesn't actually make that much difference. Like trying to clean up a litre of spilt milk with a cotton bud.

Personally, I blame them. The crazy family.

Right now, I am sitting in the chicken shed on my own. Apart from the chickens. It's a good place to sit and think and try to work out where it all went wrong. And wait. Chickens don't judge. But they are good listeners.

Well, obviously, they don't understand, but they do all the other things that good listeners do. Like nod. And not make totally stupid comments or do something grossly gross, like my brothers. And not say, "You should write it down as a story,

Becca – you'll feel so much better," like my dad. And not suddenly shout, "Got it!" and run out of the room muttering numbers and scattering bits of wire and pieces of not-quite-finished inventions, like my mum.

Let me explain. Back to the day it began, about ten days ago. Only ten days? It feels like for ever.

When I switched on my computer that afternoon, there was an email from Stella. You can rely on Stella. The jars in her kitchen even have labels telling you what's in them. I don't think my parents ever went in Stella's house. If they had, they might have learnt something about being organized. Things might go right in this house for a change.

Seeing her email address there made me wish I could go back to that time. The Stella time. When we lived in wonderful, noisy, smelly London and I knew where I was and I didn't have to THINK about things and WORRY.

Little did I know that not long after the email from Stella, when all the bad stuff happened, I'd be wishing for the Stella time even more. But I'm getting ahead of myself. First, the email.

You aren't supposed to take any notice of spelling and stuff like that in emails, by the way. Email is not like real life. It's a lot more relaxing.

From: Stella
To: Becca

Hi Bec!!!!!!!!!! How r u?
U r SOOOOOOOOOO lucky not going to
school! 2day Beetroot made us learn three
French verbs all in one day. He said he had this
brill way of learning (NOT!!!) and we had 2 close
our iiiiis and think about something reeeelly
relaaaaaaaaaaaaaaaxing and then the verbs
would just go into our heads just like that. God it
woz SOOOOOOOOOO boring and it didn't even
work. Well, Creepy Crawly Clarey said it did but
u no wot she's like!!!!
Have u made any new friends? U better not
4get me, your BEST friend. How r your horrible
brothers? And has your mum killed anyone with
her inventions yet??????!!!!!!!
We r going on a geography field trip somewhere.
Some kind of alternative farm – maybe it's near
u? Don't know where but not in London. Creepy
Crawly Clarey asked if there would be any
Vietnamese pot-bellied pigs. Sarah said, why –
r u hoping to see your relatives? Beetroot made
Sarah stay in at lunch cos of that.
Email me back soon.
Love
Stella the Star xx

I could see her in my head. I could see her thick brown hair, the colour of dark chocolate. I could see the freckles that she hates and which I always pretend I haven't noticed. I could see her *South Park* pencil case with the label saying *Stella the Star*, from the whole set of labels she got for Christmas about three years ago and was still using, even though we were at senior school now, because Stella doesn't care about growing out of things or something being too babyish. Stella's too kind of, I don't know, CONFIDENT to worry about things like that. And although I couldn't see inside her pencil case, I knew that it would have everything you needed in it. And spares in case someone needed to borrow something. There would even be a spare protractor. Not even Creepy Crawly Clarey had two protractors. Stella is very well organized. It is one of the best things about her because you just know that everything will work out when she is in charge.

I really really wished she was here with me and we could sit in my room with music on, and we could just talk and laugh about stuff. And I wouldn't ever have to explain anything. Or hide anything. Stella knows everything about me. I even wished I'd been there when Beetroot did his stupid new French verb learning thing. His real name is Mr Beathopper, by the way, in case you were thinking that someone could never really be called Mr Beetroot.

I emailed her back straightaway.

From:	Becca
To:	Stella

Hi Stell!!!!!!! How r u?????!!!
Thanks 4 the email. Wot is Beetroot ON?
Sounds like the sort of thing my dad would do.
Having lessons from my parents is kind of
weerrrrd. But we havent really had that much.
They said we dont have 2 follow normal terms
and holidays. My dad said "Education is open-
ended." That means it doesn't stop 4 holidays.
Sounds gr8, huh?
I've got my own laptop now tho!!!!!!
COOOOOOL. It's got the Internet and its in my
room so my stinking brothers can't get at it.
Makes up for the lack of mobile. Mum made me
a lock for my door. I can't use it tho becos its
electronic and its not quite right yet. I told her I
could just have a bolt or a key like normal
people but she said it's more fun to have an
electronic one. Even if it doesnt work. She is
mad. Some things never change. Why can't I
have sensible parents like yours??????????
Do you think being crazy is inherited? God, what

if I turn out like them? Help, Stell! Get me out of here!

I hope your farm trip is near here. There are farms everywhere. I don't know what people do in them all day. I only ever see cows and things just hanging around.

I've seen 2 girls I might be friends with. They come past our house sometimes. They look nice. COURSE I wont 4get u!!!!!

My room is cool. And the house is massive. Almost so big I dont have to see my brothers for the whole day. I wish u could come and see it. Can u come in the holidays? You could get a train and we could meet u. It would be so cool. We have practically a whole river running through the garden. And there's a barn thing that I can have for myself, like a studio or something. And I am going to grow things in the greenhouse. I might use them to make organic face-packs and herbal bath bombs and stuff. I could be a businesswoman! I could be rich!

Got 2 go. Mum's calling.

Loadsa luv,

Bec

Ps we're getting the chickens soon!!!

Do you think they'll be crazy too??

Mum wasn't calling, but uncomfortable thoughts were coming into my head. Massive house? Cool? All this "life is great" stuff. Who was I kidding? Why couldn't I tell Stella the truth? Because thinking about it was too hard? Yes, but also, actually, because I am not a moaning-whining-whingeing sort of a person. Nor is Stella. That's why I don't moan to her. Usually, I'm quite a jokey person. Stella and I laugh about anything and everything. But lately, I've become a bit more of a worrier. Sometimes, this sort of mouldy, foggy feeling goes through me and I just feel, well, cloudy? Mouldy? I don't know, but one of them anyway. Or maybe both.

Don't worry – most of the time, I'm fine. Cracking jokes like Great-aunt Margie's face-powder, that's me. But just then, for once, I didn't want to crack jokes with Stella. I wanted to tell her the truth.

The truth? Moving house has made me feel definitely mouldy-cloudy. Grey. You're supposed to feel blue, I know, but I feel definitely grey. A drizzly colour. I had been looking forward to everything: the excitement, the bigger house, the new room, all that. The massive garden that you could hide in. Chickens. I wasn't to know how it would make me feel. I suppose the truth is I'm homesick. But this is supposed to be home now.

13

After I'd clicked Send, I also had this uncomfortable feeling that maybe I wasn't ready for Stella to come. Not just yet. Mainly, I didn't want her to see I didn't have any friends.

She would feel sorry for me if she saw I didn't have any friends. I hate people feeling sorry for me.

But at the same time I have to admit I felt sorry for myself. Even a bit panicky. What if I NEVER made friends? It's difficult when you've only moved house a few weeks before. It's especially difficult when you don't go to school. I don't think I've ever had to make new friends before. They were always just "there". Even when I started at secondary school, before we came here, I moved to the same school with all my old friends. And they knew about me and ... everything, and my parents and my brothers, and some of them had even been in our kitchen and survived. I didn't have to explain anything. There is something I haven't told you yet. Because I... I don't know. I just haven't. It's just that I don't... Maybe later. Definitely later. I promise.

But how would I make friends? What would they think of my family? And me? I mean there's nothing exactly wrong with me – like, I don't have two heads or anything – but I just think, why would anyone CHOOSE to be friends with me?

I'm quite ordinary. Boring. I am nothing in particular. You wouldn't say, "Oh yes, Becca, the one with the seriously cool hair," or "The one who's amazing at gymnastics?" or "Oh yeah, the one with the gorgeous brother." You'd be more likely to say, "Who? No, I can't picture her."

I guess you might say, "Oh yeah – her. The one with the seriously weird family." And then you'd just think about something totally different and forget about me immediately. Which, actually, would be a good idea because I don't want to be "the one with the seriously weird family".

I never thought about all this before. Never wondered what I was like. I was just me. But now I had to be a me that someone else would choose to be friends with. And what sort of a me was needed for that? Not this one, for sure. Not the boring one.

Another very massive disadvantage when it comes to making friends is the totally weird and embarrassing family that I have already mentioned. You'll see what I mean. They have their good points, but right now I can't think what they are. And anyway, they tend not to show them in public, and it's pointless to have good points that you only show in private.

Anyway, as I was saying to Stella, I'd seen two girls walk past our house on their way home from school each day. I'd seen them look over the gate. They probably wanted to see the new people who live at Brook House. I could be friends with them, I thought. They looked ... well, I don't know. They looked definitely cool. A bit scary maybe, but then people you don't know always are. One of the girls had mega-unreal black hair with a pink streak in it. Maybe their school didn't have a uniform – if it did, they didn't seem to wear it. Unless the school rule was you just had to wear black. Some schools have uniforms that are black – but I don't think a black top with a silver axe on it would quite come into it. You could tell they took a lot of trouble over how they looked. I would have to have more clothes and take more trouble if I wanted to be friends with them. I did want to be friends with them. I really did.

They were definitely not boring.

If you were talking about them, you would say, "Oh, yeah I know those two. The seriously cool and trendy ones. With the hair."

They didn't look like Stella. I know I shouldn't say it but they looked cooler, trendier. They looked as though they would be majorly popular. Not that Stella isn't. But Stella just looks normal and nice. If you looked at Stella, you wouldn't immediately think, wow, how AMAZING to be her friend. With these girls you would.

16

I didn't think Stella would like them. But I was the one who needed friends right then.

I had a mental picture of how I could make friends with them. I would be in the garden, hanging around, dressed in my newest jeans etc, and they would see me and shout, "Hiya" and I would shout, "Hiya" back and ask them if they wanted to come in. And that would be that. New friends, straightaway. And I wouldn't tell them the private thing about me at first. I don't like telling people. I find it completely boring. I would need to know them better before I would tell them. Maybe after a week.

It almost happened like that. At first. Basically, that same afternoon, I was in the front garden, wearing the coolest clothes I had. We don't have enough money for me to have stacks of new clothes, but my jeans were just about new enough and I do seriously *do* accessories. Accessories are my thing, especially jewellery. I collect accessories, big time. I am going to be a jewellery designer and I am going to have a shop in Bond Street, London. Definitely.

Anyway, there I was, casually lying in the sun, as though that's what someone who doesn't go to school does all day. (That is completely NOT the case.) I was wearing sunglasses, so I could watch

17

the lane while pretending to be asleep, and my handbag earrings. (These are earrings that look like designer handbags with Marilyn Monroe on them. You need to look quite closely to see that that's who it is, though.) And there they were, walking slowly along and stopping at our fence. That was my cue to wake up casually and act surprised. Which I did.

"Hiya!" I called.

"Hiya!" one of them called back. They walked through the gate and towards me. So far so good.

Then my mum came out of the house. With my four-year-old twin brothers. And an invention. My heart sank. I knew what it was. It was her invention for putting duvet covers on. Yes, I know – uh?? No, I hadn't realized there was any big deal with putting duvet covers on either, but apparently there was. So she had invented a contraption for sorting out the problem and now she was going to test it. In the front garden. With my brothers helping. And those girls watching.

"Um, Mum!" I called, to alert her to the presence of visitors. "These two girls have called by."

"Oh, hello!" she smiled at them. "Pleased to meet you. Would one of you hold this corner, please?" The girls just stood there, looking disgusted, as though someone had asked them to clean out a toilet or something.

Let me know if your mum does things like that and I'll come round to explain the exact and precise and totally clear meaning of the word *embarrassment* to her.

"Mum, don't be so embarrassing. You can't ask guests to do that!" I said quickly, rolling my eyes at the girls. One of them smiled. Well, maybe it was more a sneer than a smile. But I wasn't in the mood for analysing smile levels. I fiddled with my handbag earrings, to make sure they were the right way up. And to make sure they would see them.

I looked at the pink streak on the black-haired girl. Then I noticed it was an add-on. Still pretty amazing, though, even if it was fake. In fact, I was glad it wasn't real. If it had been real, I'd have felt even more boring. They both held mobile phones in their hands.

My four-year-old twin brothers were staring at the girls. One was picking his nose. They both started fiddling with the contraption and pulling it in two directions. They don't stand still for long. Mum looked at the girls and smiled in a wispy, vague sort of way, as though she wasn't completely on the same planet. (Sometimes it would be better if she was not, though she can be quite generous with money if she's not paying attention, which is usually, even though we are not rich.)

"No, sorry, of course not," she said. "Never mind, you can help me later, Becca. Come on boys, let's get this road on the show," and she moved towards an empty part of the lawn and started climbing into the duvet cover.

Yes, I did say that.

I did warn you.

It was essential that I should get those girls somewhere where they couldn't see anyone from my family.

"Do you want to come in?" I asked, half wishing they would say no and then they could just go and we could start again another day. And I would make sure there were no loony members of my family within embarrassment distance.

"Cool," said the one with the pink streak. I was fascinated by the clever wildness of her hair. It hung around her face and clung to her cheeks with bits like fingers at the side. One strand went right over her eyes and she didn't even brush it away. The other girl had hundreds of blonde braids. Well, dozens anyway. They both wore lip-gloss. I *have* lip-gloss, obviously, but I don't wear it in the middle of the day. My boringness was growing by the second. Image was definitely seeming more important by the minute.

Anyway, the girls wanted to come in.

Luckily, Dad was out, so we could safely go in

the house. Not the kitchen, though. You haven't seen our kitchen. There are jars that have tadpoles painted on them because they used to have tadpoles in but now have either moss or green mould, and other jars with beansprouts sprouting everywhere, and empty baked bean tins joined by string, and bits of my brothers' artwork, and one of the cupboard doors is completely covered in a pasta collage in the shape of the Eiffel Tower, even though we've only lived here a few weeks.

I needed to get them up to my room without them seeing the kitchen. Or the sitting room. Or the hall. Everywhere was still full of packing cases and things that were not where they would be in a normal house.

Sometimes, I think I need a separate door for friends. Or a separate house. It was the same when we lived in London. But people knew us then. It didn't matter. Well, actually, often it did matter, but not so much.

I wished I was back in London. I suddenly even wished I was at school. It would all be so much simpler.

Now, of course, ten days later, sitting in the chicken shed as darkness falls around me, I wish I hadn't asked those girls to come in. But I wasn't to know that then. I was happy for anyone to want to come in. To be honest, I would even have let an axe murderer's daughters in if I'd thought they might be my friends.

Friends Already

We safely negotiated the stairs, which looked as though we'd been burgled, and I led the way to my room.

It is a brilliant room. I've made it mine already and it smells of me and my things, not the strangers who used to live here. It's right up at the top of the house, away from everyone else, and it's got loads of sloping ceilings. The carpet's all right. It's got a stain on it that I am trying not to think about, so I've put a rug over it. And Mum painted it for me – the room, not the carpet – in a bright yellow colour I chose myself. She didn't put enough paint on some bits because she had to rush off to deal with an idea that had just sprung into her head, but I can always put posters over those. I've started sticking some of my best artwork up already.

The girl with blonde braids looked round. "I'm

Jazz, by the way," she said. "You're Becca. I heard your mum say." She seemed friendly enough. She was much prettier than me. She looked at herself in the mirror quite a lot, just to make sure she was still as pretty as the last time she looked. She was. You would definitely say, "Oh, yes, Jazz! That really pretty one? With the hair?"

The other one sat down in front of my computer. I hoped she wouldn't see my chicken project on the desk. She was so confident, it was awesome. I would never sit down in someone else's house before they told me to. That's probably me being boring again. I really need to stop being so boring.

"What's your name?" I asked her.

"Mel." She didn't look at me. She put her mobile phone on the desk in front of her. I noticed her black nail varnish. Her black T-shirt had "wot u lookin at?" written on the back of it. I felt I had to look away, that she might be able to see out of the back of her head or something. She didn't seem to be able to keep still. Then she spun the swivel chair round and round with her feet sticking out. I was just waiting for her to knock a photo frame off my bedside table. She didn't, but she easily could have done.

"Can I see your CDs?" asked Jazz, who had just finished checking her face in the mirror. Now, if there's one thing I am proud of, it's my collection

24

of CDs. All set out in rows along three shelves of a bookcase.

"Cool collection!" said Jazz. When she said that, I can't tell you how I felt. Like walking onto warm sand with bare feet. Or like licking lemon sherbet ice cream that's just beginning to melt. That describes what it was like to me, anyway. My dad says I should be a writer. There's no way I would be a writer. Ever. You have to hang around the house all day and be weird. Also, on television once I saw a writer who sat around so much that she got a thing called deep-vein thrombosis, which is where a lump of blood forms in your leg because you've been sitting in a chair all day, and then it goes all the way through your veins with a terrible dramatic shooting pain, and when it gets to your lungs you die. My dad is paranoid about deep-vein thrombosis and he stands up every hour and jogs up and down the stairs four times, pumping his arms and breathing deeply and loudly. Or, if he's too busy to do that, he wears thick elastic stockings, which are gross. They are even seriously unfashionable for grown-ups. And that's saying something when you have a father who wears socks with sandals, and jeans that will always be exactly the opposite of what is fashionable at the time. He also has a saggy cardigan, but I have just about trained him not to wear that, except when he is safely hidden from public view.

Anyway, Mel jumped off the chair and picked out a CD. "Yeah, cool," she said, and I could have grinned but I managed to keep it in. "I've got all theirs. Can we listen to this one?" she asked.

She was flipping the CD into the CD player before I'd had time reply. I decided I liked Jazz more than Mel. I was a bit scared of Mel. But I wanted Mel to like me. Even more than I wanted Jazz to like me, somehow. Even though Jazz was nicer. Why was that?

I needed to get to know Mel better, I told myself. Then it would be fine. She was only scary because I didn't know her. She was cool, really, I could tell that. And if I was more like her, I would not be boring any more.

Jazz was looking at a photo of Stella. She didn't say anything but I could sort of sense her judging.

The music filled the room. Mel turned the volume up. The bass vibrated through my body and made my bones feel like chalk on a blackboard. I told myself to relax. It was a big house, after all. No one would hear. And anyway, it was only music. You're allowed to play music loudly in your own house. You will only NOT do that if you are very boring or if you haven't got your parents under control.

"So, what school you go to?" asked Jazz. "We

never seen you. You go to boarding school or what?" She put her mobile by Stella's photo. It was exactly the sort I wish I had.

"I don't go to school," I said.

"How cool is *that*!" said Mel in a strangely loud voice, as though she was in a play and the audience was out there listening. But I had obviously impressed her. She looked at me in a genuinely interested sort of way. "How come? You get chucked out? My brother got chucked out. Booze. And other stuff. He's eighteen." She sounded quite proud. She pushed one of her cuticles back and held her black fingernails up to the light.

"Nah," I said, as casually as I could, flicking my hair back and playing with my handbag earrings, which they still hadn't noticed. "My parents don't like schools. They don't like rules."

"Oh, right! Like we really believe you!" Mel grinned. "All parents like rules."

"Not mine," I said.

"Cool," said Mel. "Your parents are cool."

A smile melted all the way down to my stomach. Like strawberry cheesecake. Like honey cream.

(I'm still not going to be a writer.)

You probably think I was totally stupid to think they were my type. Well, I suppose if I'd thought

27

about it properly, I *did* know deep down that they weren't my type. But I thought if I changed, I could be *their* type. That was what I wanted. There was definitely something about them that was what I wanted to be. Cool. Not caring much. Interesting. Not boring. Someone you'd remember in a crowd. Unlike me.

I suddenly wished my room was painted black instead of yellow. Or at least had something black in it. I thought that Mel would think that was cool. She would respect black but not yellow. Somehow I knew that.

"Did you do those?" asked Mel, pointing at one of my designs on the wall. It was a picture of some really way-out Manolo Blahnik-style shoes.

"Yeah," I said. I flicked my hair back again and caught sight of myself in a mirror. I reached for some lip-gloss buried somewhere in a drawer. "I'm going to be a shoe designer one day." You couldn't actually wear shoes like that, though. Not if you didn't want to do serious damage to your feet.

"You couldn't wear shoes like that," said Jazz.

"Don't be so stupid," said Mel. "It's called art."

"You should be an artist," said Jazz. "Those are totally cool."

Yes, I could be an artist. That sounded like a really good and unboring idea.

The lip-gloss was a major improvement.

28

By now, I'd just about run out of things to say. I wanted to ask them questions, but the questions in my head sounded boring. Like, "Do you have any pets?" "What do you like doing at school?" They were the sort of questions a polite relative would ask if they hadn't seen you since you were five and they were trying desperately to show how incredibly good they were at talking to young people. I thought maybe I should ask if Mel and Jazz wanted something to eat, but I so did *not* want to take them into the kitchen. That would be extremely risky. It made me sweat even to think about it.

Jazz picked up her mobile phone. You could tell it was new. You could tell from the way she held it, carefully, and looked at it a lot. She held it slightly away from her body, as though showing it to me without actually wanting to look as though she was showing it to me.

I knew what she was going to ask even before she asked it. "What's your number?" she asked. "I can add you to my address book."

"Um, I'm between phones," I replied. They both looked at me. Wide-eyed. Then they looked at each other. And back at me.

"What? You mean you haven't got one?" Mel's voice was amazed. And scornful, I knew that.

"Oh, I *had* one," I said. "I've had a phone for

like *ages*. But something happened to it and I haven't quite got a new one yet. I'm getting one for my birthday. A really cool one."

"I broke mine once. Got a new one on insurance. Why didn't you do that?" Jazz asked.

"Because the insurance people said that what happened to mine was definitely not an accident."

"Oh, like you did it on purpose so you could get a new one? *Cool!* My dad said that sort of stuff is stealing!" said Mel, maybe thinking that my criminal tendencies made me a suitable friend for her.

"No, just that they didn't see how tomato ketchup could get inside by mistake."

They looked at me. "Your brothers?" asked Jazz.

"Why?" asked Mel.

"There doesn't need to be a reason with brothers," said Jazz wisely.

"Actually, there was a reason," I said. I paused. "Mum had told them that computers and mobile phones, and things like that, all have chips inside them. So my brothers got my phone and dropped it on the floor to get the back off. They were cross when they couldn't find any chips, so they put ketchup inside it. Not logical, I know, but that's how their brains work. When the insurance company said they wouldn't replace it, Mum cleaned it up and showed my brothers what all the bits were for. That's how her brain works. Then my dad wrote a story about it. That's how his brain works."

"God, your family really are weird. My mum would just go ballistic and swear a lot and then buy me a new one," said Mel.

I wished I hadn't told them so much detail. I should just have said my phone was being repaired or something. They didn't need to know too much about my family all at once.

Anyway, just then I heard Mum calling that it was tea-time. I rolled my eyes and pretended I was sorry they had to go. They picked up their phones. On the way out, we met my brothers. They stared at the girls. Mel and Jazz looked at them as though they were disgusting. My brothers often are disgusting, but I don't particularly like anyone else noticing. Stella can because she is Stella, but no one else. It's not at all cool to have gross brothers.

"Gross," said Mel loudly to Jazz as we walked on.

"Grosser," agreed Jazz.

"Most gross," sneered Mel. "Poor you, having to live with those!"

"Yeah, life sucks," I replied, scowling at my brothers.

"Why's your mouth all wet?" said one to me.

"Why's your brain wet?" I replied. They stuck out their tongues.

"Prob'ly dribbling," said the other.

"Dribbling wibbling," said the first one.

"Don't worry," said Jazz to me. "We'll look after you."

"Yeah," said Mel, linking arms with me. "We'll protect you from that grossness. Get lost, little boys," she said. "Or you're dead."

It was just a joke. It didn't mean anything. Just one of those things you say. My heart swelled and my head sang as we linked arms. These were my new friends. I had actually made friends already! Stella would be proud of me, wouldn't she?

After I'd shown the girls out and they'd promised to come back tomorrow and I'd said great and everything, I went back up to my room. Bubbling excitement made me grin. I looked in the mirror and took off the lip-gloss. Maybe there was a colder shivery feeling too, like walking into a cellar and looking back to make sure the door hasn't shut, but that might just be me imagining it now, as I think back. At the time, I am sure I just felt good. And if there were any doubts, I suppose it's hardly surprising – I was changing after all, wasn't I? It's not that easy becoming less boring. And also, making new friends is tiring. You have to try so hard all the time.

I kept the earrings on. Earrings are me, even if Mel and Jazz never noticed them.

I tidied up the things on my desk and put everything back as it had been before. I put a different CD on and went online to email Stella. There was a message from her. Stella made me feel warm and yellow inside. Even seeing her email address did it.

From: Stella
To: Becca

Hi Bec
How r u? Thanks 4 your msg. Chickens!!!!!!!!
Your family always do mad things. I wish I could
have chickens but you no wot my mum would
say! "council by-law number 86756453b(c),"
she'd say. And "think of the mess and the smell,
Stell".
I asked about coming 2 c u in the holz and my
mum and dad said that would b great. Mum is
looking up about trains and things. The farm we
are going 2 is not near u. I asked. Bad luck! u
won't c your friend Stella till later.
Your house sounds brill. Hope u make friends
with those girls. But don't worry – u will make
friends. My mum said Becca could make friends
with a spiny anteater if she wanted.
It's the holidays soon. Can't wait. We r doing all

the usual end-of-term stuff and Mrs D is getting
very excited about sports day. I'm going 2 b
throwing the javelin. Make sure ur brothers r not
in the way!
Tell me about your mum's inventions. I love
hearing about them. She is SOOOOOO clever! I
love the way u tell me the stories about them. U
could be a writer
Gotta go. Homework, worse luck!
Stell xx

I replied straightaway.

From: Becca
To: Stella

Hi Stell!!
Guess wot – I have made friends with those
girls! They are called Jazz and Mel and they r
really nice. You would like them. Jazz has
amazing braids in hr hair. Mel has a pink streak
in hr hair – just fake tho!
Well, u asked about my mum's inventions. Do
you really wanta know? Just now it's a brain-
drain chair and a duvet-cover-putting-on thing.
The duvet thing is rubbish but the chair is clever
tho useless. Yesterday I went to call her for tea
and she was totally upside down in it. Its

supposed to put more blood in your head. You sit
normally most of the time but every hour it tips u
upside down and hangs u there for 1 min
(there's a timer but that's a problem just now)
before swinging u back again. She says office
people will be queing up (help, how do u spell
that???) 2 buy it when they see how important it
is to have lots of blood in your head.
She wants to write to the Goverment 2 tell them
2 make it a law that every company should have
brain-drain chairs for their workers. But my dad
reminded her we don't approve of rules, and she
said it was different when the rule was good for
u, and my dad said no it wasnt and she would
have to come up with a better way of selling her
brain-drain chair
So! that's all the invention news. Oh, there's
some robot thing as well, but no one's allowed to
see. Could be 4 a brother's birthday.
Jazz and Mel are coming again 2morrow. I still
wish u were here of course. U could b friends
with them 2. And the chickens are coming
2morrow 2. Mel says her brother got chucked
out of school. Gotta go – chicken project has to
be finished NOW! Bad as school!!
Say hello to your mum from me.
Love
Beccccccca xx

PS well done about the javelin! I bet you win.
Remember when you threw that stick so high
into the conker tree that it went right over? No
one could believe it!

When I read it back to myself before sending it, I could almost feel I was back home again. In the Stella time. The old me, just as I was with Stella. Egg-yolk-yellow, cotton-wool-soft and chicken-soup-warm.

Now, as I sit on the dusty floor of the chicken shed, with my knees hugged up to my chin, I wonder why I ever thought I had to change the way I was.

Why couldn't everything just have stayed the same? Why did they make me change? I blame them. Mel and Jazz.

Some Explanations

There are some things I need to explain. Some of them I can't explain yet, but I want to fill you in on stuff like why I don't go to school. And I also want you to know about my brothers. You need to know that, although they are very annoying and often quite disgusting, I do actually like them. They can even be quite cute. When they are asleep. I do, in fact, quite like looking at their faces when they are asleep.

The not-going-to-school business is because of something called *civil liberties*. My mum and dad are very keen on civil liberties. It means that you shouldn't have to follow rules. Except when your parents make the rules. That's different, of course. I tried pointing that out once. What did I get? A lecture, as usual.

Anyway, what happened was this: yet again the school had called me Rebecca instead of Becca. It may seem like a small thing but, as far as Dad was concerned, it was "the final straw in the absolute giant of all straw bales". I am always called Becca, but the school computer had a problem with that and sometimes my parents would get letters where the computer had written "your daughter, Rebecca". Then my dad would say, "I feel a letter coming on." He often feels letters coming on. Not just to the school, but lots of other people who he thinks *infringe civil liberties*.

I don't want you to think that my parents are completely off their trolleys. If I tell you some of the other annoying crimes which my school committed, then you will see that there is *some* sense to my mum and dad. Not a lot, but enough to keep the men in white coats away for a while longer.

First, there was uniform. The school said uniform "promoted a sense of belonging and personal pride". My parents said uniform "turned everyone into robots and removed individuality and creative self-expression".

Then there was Mr Turner the maths teacher. Mr Turner was a truly rubbish teacher. When my parents complained that Mr Turner was not managing to explain maths to me properly at all, even though I used to be good at it, the school said that Mr Turner was a very respected teacher with thirty-five years' experience. My parents said Mr Turner was a very old teacher who had lost the will to live, let alone teach.

Then there was the time when the Duchess of somewhere visited our school. Stella and I were selected to show her round and then to present her with a massive bunch of flowers. My parents asked what educational value this had. The school said it was an honour because our school had once been called "failing" and was now called "improving" and the Duchess of somewhere was coming to congratulate us. My parents said the Duchess of somewhere "represented an outdated symbol of power and oppression" and, anyway, if she was congratulating *us*, why were we giving *her* a present and not the other way round? Who did she think she was? And who was paying for this bunch of flowers? And shouldn't the money be spent on books?

There were loads of other things, too, but I think maybe you are getting the picture. My parents seriously did not like lots of things about schools and governmenty people making rules. I definitely sympathize. They said we got too many worksheets and not enough "room for creativity". I totally agree. They said schools should "be moulded to the shape of the child, not the other way round". I am not *quite* sure what that meant.

Both those things sound weird to me.

Anyway, one morning, it all came to a head after this "Rebecca" thing. I was called to the head teacher's office. My dad was standing there with a burning look on his face. "Mrs Ballantine," he said. "I shall be making alternative provision for the education of my daughter." I could almost see electricity coming from his eyes. He practically even spat. I felt sorry for Mrs Ballantine, I really did. She seemed to shrink. And she is very small anyway.

Alternative provision. My dad uses words like that because he is a writer. (His sort of writing does not actually use long words, but I think that makes him even keener to use them whenever possible. Like when talking to Mrs Ballantine.) Anyway, I did actually know what *alternative provision* meant. We take a completely different sort of alternative provision when we go to my great-aunt Margie's house, because my dad says her fridge is a danger to human health. Those provisions are packets of biscuits and dried apricots and cashew nuts. And gin. But this sort of alternative provision that my dad was talking about meant *other arrangements*.

After the meeting with Mrs Ballantine, I had to quickly collect all my things from my locker and get in the car with everyone staring out of the school windows. If there had been television cameras there at the time, I would definitely have had a blanket over my head.

Once we were in the car, my dad gripped the steering wheel and drove as fast as our car could go, which is not very. We turned down a street which was not the way home.

"We're getting the boys," muttered my dad as a sort of explanation.

I didn't ask why. I guessed I was going to find out anyway. I did. He carried on. "I'm not having them being part of this ridiculous so-called education system either. If it's not good enough for you, it's not good enough for them. Flaming rules. Flaming rules made by flaming idiots with grey suits and clipboards." I'd never seen Mrs Ballantine with a grey suit or a clipboard, but maybe my dad knew something I didn't. He carried on muttering about final straws and flaming rules and tiny minds and certain people needing to get a life.

At my brothers' nursery, my dad stormed in and then stormed out again about three minutes later with a brother on each side and a face like a cloud. He drove us home. Fast. As we jolted over the speed ramps, I had the feeling he was loving every rattling bump. His eyes blazed at every jump. The car had hardly stopped before he was flinging open the door and leaping out, shouting, "Jill! Jill! I've done it!"

I followed him through the gate and round the

side of the house to the shed at the very end of the long, thin back garden where my mum worked. She was hanging upside down in the brain-drain chair. The one-minute timer had obviously gone wrong again.

As my dad strode towards her, with me following behind, my mum suddenly swung upright and hit her head on the top of the chair.

"Sugar!" she said, her face red and puzzled, but smiling. "Still can't *quite* get that right! Why are the children home? Is it tea-time already? Goodness! I haven't prepared anything and I meant to get to the shops and I don't think there's anything worth having in the fridge. Maybe there's still some of that rice thingy we had the other day?"

"Jill, for goodness' sake, get a grip! It's only ten o'clock in the morning. My meeting. Remember? At the school? Mrs Ballantine? About Becca?"

"Becca? What's she done?"

"No, not Becca! Mrs Ballantine! The school! All of them! The system!"

My mum was looking serious now. Her face was still red but with all that blood in her brain she must have been able to concentrate especially well at that moment. Her hair, which is short and kind of a colour somewhere between fair and not so fair, depending on whether the sun is shining, was sticking up. It made her look too much like an inventor. Even though she was one. I used to like saying my mum was an inventor, but now I'd definitely rather she got a normal job. Like Stella's mum. Working for the council is normal. It makes you organized because of all the rules. When you work for the council you have rules about everything, Stella's mum says. You even have rules about the words you can use and the things you can think. You even have rules about what sort of rules you can make.

"What have you done, Seb?"

"Time for a family meeting," replied my dad, looking very determined and still fierce. "I'm going to put the kettle on. Kitchen in five." My mum calmly unhitched herself from the brain-drain chair, took the pencil out from behind her ear and peeled the piece of Blu-Tack off her forehead – she puts it there to stick screws and things into so she doesn't lose them – and followed him into the house. She didn't ask questions – she's very patient, my mum. She needs to be.

Family meetings are important in our house. We have meetings about things like why the rota for chores has completely broken down, again, or how we are determined to enjoy Christmas despite the fact that Great-aunt Margie will be there again, and will grumble and fart in the corner, and eat all the orange creams and get Brazil nuts stuck in her false teeth, and drink too much sherry and then keep telling us how the Brussels sprouts are still *repeating* on her.

My brothers were in the kitchen already. Eating biscuits. They are four, as I think I have told you. They annoy me a lot when I am in a bad mood. They make me laugh when I'm in a good mood. If it could be the other way round, there would be some point in having twin brothers.

Even though they are twins, they don't look alike. Thank goodness. That would be too obvious. I am embarrassed about their names, so I am not going to say them until you know my family a bit better. I have a normal name. But after I was born, my parents went a bit odd, according to my grandparents, though I don't think it was because I was born that they went odd.

My grandpa said they went green, which I didn't understand when he first said it but obviously now I know that it means liking vegetables that have been grown on horse manure, recycling glass in bottle banks and only using the car when you really need to. Like when you are in a hurry. Or to go to the bottle bank. Anyway, they started keeping a disgusting stinking bin in the kitchen, which we still have. We have to put our apple cores and stuff in it, and when it's full and slimy they tip it all in another stinking bin in the garden and add special worms to it, which makes it smell even more disgusting but is good for the plants. Anyway, when the twins were born, they called them... Well, as I said, later.

My mum and dad are ... different. There's nothing wrong with that, of course. I'd quite like to be different myself. But in a different way. I just wish it didn't have to be my parents who chose to be that way.

I am not going to be a writer or an inventor. I've already told you why I'm not going to be a writer. But I'm not inventor material either – you wouldn't catch me with Blu-tack stuck to my forehead to stick screws in. I would just put the screws back in their container. Or I'd have an assistant to hold them for me.

I am going to be an interior designer. I am good at art, but normal artists are even weirder than writers so I'd need to be a special type of artist that is not at all weird. I think I might have already told you I was going to be something else, but there are actually quite a lot of things I'd like to be. Anyway, it's good to have back-up jobs in case one doesn't work, or maybe gets off to a slow start, so I have quite a lot of back-up jobs. One is a scientist. I would find cures for as many illnesses as I can. Starting with diabetes. I don't know why that one, particularly. It just came into my head.

Anyway, back to that family meeting.

We all sat round the kitchen table. It's a round table, so no one can sit at the head of it. But you still always get the feeling that my mum and dad are sitting at each end. I don't know how they do that, but it's one of the annoying things about them.

One of my brothers, the taller, skinnier one with specs, was picking at a splintery bit of the table. He looks like a small Harry Potter, except that he has fair hair which sticks up. The other one has slightly darker hair which is flat instead of sticking-up. He was sitting perfectly still, except for his head – it kept moving, from mum to dad and back again. Sometimes it's my dad who starts and sometimes it's my mum. I knew it would be my dad this time. I could see it in his face, burning a hole in his eyes with trying to get out.

And out it came. Like a bullet. Not that a bullet would ever come *out* of someone's head. But maybe more like *projectile vomiting*. I know about projectile vomiting because L— one of my brothers, the Harry Potterish one, had it when he was a baby. I remember it. You don't easily forget projectile vomiting.

"I have withdrawn Becca from school and taken the boys from nursery," said Dad. Just like that.

You'd think my mum would be shocked. Most

mums would be, I imagine. But not mine. She just sort of very slowly, as though she was trying to deal tactfully with an angry lion which might attack her if she said the wrong thing or just said it in the wrong voice, said, "Ri–i–i–ight," in a way that had four separate syllables in it and went up at the end to make it like a question.

That was all my dad needed. Out it all came like a waterfall, or something else rushing and loud. I can't remember all of it, but it was mostly about the school not respecting pupils and how Mrs Ballantine was a dried-up old bat who wouldn't recognize civil liberties if they came up and bit her on the nose. I remember one part where apparently Mrs Ballantine had said, "I am sorry, Mr Jarrett, really very sorry, but is it so important? After all, Rebecca is her real name. It is on her birth certificate." And he had said, "No, Mrs Ballantine, she is *called* Becca. Her birth certificate is irrelevant. It is merely information by which the Government controls its citizens. And besides, imagine if Becca chose to call you Hilda." Mrs Ballantine had said that would be different. My dad had asked why. And Mrs Ballantine had said, "Because Rebecca is a child and I am an adult, and that is just the way the world works." And my dad had said something like, "Ah, so it's one of those 'because I say so' situations, is it HILDA?" I can't remember what Mrs Ballantine had said then but that was when my dad asked her to arrange for me to be called to her office. And when I arrived he said this thing about making alternative provision for my education. "And I can tell you I don't regret it one bit," he finished, staring at my mum.

She took a sip of her tea. "Well, Seb, I know we discussed it, of course. But I did think we were going to leave it till the end of term and … um … investigate it a little more." Oh? So they had discussed this already, had they? So much for family meetings.

"What is 'altervatin provisial'?" asked my brother who doesn't look like Harry Potter.

"Alternative provision. It means you won't be going to nursery any more and you won't be going to school after the summer," said Mum.

Then the Harry Potter one choked on his biscuit and had to be bashed on the back by Mum and she had something black – machine oil, or Marmite, you can never tell in our kitchen – on her hand and it went all over his blue sweatshirt. That gave me some time to think.

"You mean, not at all?" I asked my dad. This did not seem normal. I knew I was awake because everything else seemed completely normal. For us. But I thought you had to go to school until you were nearly grown-up and then you didn't have to do anything you were told any more. Which couldn't come too soon, if you'd asked me.

"Yes, not at all," he said, with a weird sort of bright smile that went right through his eyes. As though something was shining inside his head. You know? Like when you shine a torch through your hand and it glows red with all the blood? "Not at all. Not ever. What do you think of that?"

"Sounds... I don't know. Are we allowed? Isn't it against the rules?"

"You and your rules, Becca!" he said. "Anyway, there's no rule that says you have to go to school. The rule just says parents have to 'provide an adequate education'. I checked. It's just that most people get schools to do it for them. Maybe they can't think of a better way to educate their children. Well, I can! We will do it ourselves!"

I was trying to sort out two thoughts that were happening in my head at the same time. First, not going to school. That meant things like not having to get up early, not wearing school uniform, and not having to put up with boys spitting. And not being pushed around in the lunch queue just because you were wearing the wrong label, or your schoolbag was a brand that no sportsperson would be seen dead promoting. But second, being taught by my parents. How would they know what to teach us? They didn't know ANY of the right things. Neither of them knew anything about *tundral environments*, which is what we were doing in geography just then. And they couldn't speak French at all – we had gone to France once, and every time they tried to ask for something in French, the French people had looked at them in disbelief and said, "May I help you?" in perfect English. They couldn't even teach the things they were supposed to know about, like English (my dad) and physics (my mum), because they would insist on telling me completely irrelevant things and going off into huge long boring lectures, instead of just telling me the answer to the question on my homework sheet.

But, I have to admit, it's amazing what adults can do when they want to. I really did think you had to go to school, but it turned out my dad was right. Anyway, as you know very well by now, I didn't go back to school and we moved house. We left London and came to live here, in the West Country, just outside the village of Midwinter and not near anywhere I'd ever heard of before.

Why did we have to move to the country as well as leaving school? Several reasons. Dad said we needed a fresh start, a challenge, a complete change of lifestyle. He also said that having a bus going past his desk every day was very distracting when he was writing his children's TV scripts – oh, now I've told you what he writes and you can see it's not very cool. To get the full picture of how completely uncool this is, you need to imagine him acting out the part of odd aliens with high-pitched voices and stupid prongs on their heads, and silly storylines involving vegetables or talking dustbins. He also once wrote a series about two pigs that sailed round the world in a paddling pool, and a journalist even came to our house to interview him, and my whole family, including me, had to be photographed actually sitting in a paddling pool. And everyone said how cute my brothers looked but why did they have flowerpots on their heads? I expect you are now getting the idea.

Anyway, he said that when he was sitting at his desk, people kept looking at him from the top deck of the bus and sometimes even waving. Which was disturbing his so-called *creative flow*. My mum said she needed a bigger shed for all her inventions, and a bigger garden to test them in. She said it would be safer. Dad agreed. So did I.

They both said the country was more educational than the city. I don't get that at all. There aren't more books or anything. There's more nature, I suppose. And cows. So what? There's not really anything educational about cows that I can see.

They also said they could do their work equally well in the country.

Dad said he'd always wanted to keep chickens.

At one point they paused to ask what I thought. I said something about liking it in London. They said I could have a laptop if we moved. That changed things a lot. That and the idea of a big house and a new bedroom. And chickens. For some reason, I liked the idea of chickens. Call me boring if you want.

I admit I did become very excited about moving. It was great being the centre of attention, and everyone at school signed a card and gave me presents. That was before I thought about it properly. Especially the friends thing. Well, I wasn't to know how hard it would be. My parents should have known. That's the sort of thing parents are supposed to know about.

So, anyway, the thing with Mrs Ballantine was how it all began. I could blame Mrs B and all the people with their "flaming rules and clipboards" for all the bad stuff that happened afterwards. Or I could blame my parents for making us move without really consulting me properly. Even though I probably would have voted for moving. But as I sit here in the chicken shed alone, I am beginning to wonder if it is really fair to blame any of them.

Chickens

Just in case you think that not going to school means not doing any work, think again. That same day that Jazz and Mel called round, the day before the chickens were coming, I had to finish my project. As soon as I'd finished emailing Stella, I set to work.

The chicken project was very important to me. This is not because I am some kind of boring swot. It's because I had put myself in charge of the chickens. I knew I was the only one responsible enough. I was the one who had been on the Internet to research the different breeds of chickens and find out which ones are the easiest to keep. There wasn't a special sort recommended for families who are very scatty and might forget to feed them, but I would make sure the chickens got fed. I considered making a rota. But the twins couldn't be on the rota. When I asked them if they knew what chickens ate, one of them said, "eggs". That's a very disgusting idea, if you think about it.

My project was called *All You Need to Know About Chickens.* Before we left London, an inspector person had come round to tell my parents how they should teach us. This inspector had brought round so many booklets and leaflets and folders and documents that I almost had a fit. Then I realized they weren't for me, which was a massive relief.

They were for Mum and Dad. They had to read them ALL. Imagine watching your parents doing homework. That's what it was like. Brilliant! Mum even had her tongue stuck out, she had to concentrate so hard. Anyway, they both sat up most of the night reading this mountain of words.

And the next day, you would think they had been qualified teachers for about a million years. They used very important-sounding words, like "strands" and "outcomes" and "learning objectives". To be honest, I thought they were taking it MUCH too seriously.

Then, they took no notice of any of it anyway. "We'll adapt it," they said confidently. "We will follow that thing on the Internet called – what was it? – *integrated holistic learning.*" I think this means basically "a whole lot of learning all lumped together and mixed up".

The result of all this was that they set me the most incredibly huge chicken assignment that covered every part of every subject you've ever heard of and I was given weeks to finish it in. It was like being back at primary school.

This was what I had to do:

- Investigate:
  1. the history of chickens and their role in society since the Middle Ages;
  2. the environmental benefits of keeping chickens;
  3. the geography of chicken breeds around the world;
  4. the care and maintenance of chickens.
- Find examples of chickens in stories and cultures from different countries.
- Compare the cost of keeping different types of chickens and work out how many eggs each would have to lay for us to make a profit.
- Find chicken recipes and investigate their role in a healthy diet.
- Write a "Day in the Life of a Chicken" diary.
- Write a poem where each line begins with the letters that make up the word "chicken".
- Draw a chicken using charcoal shading;

and another one in silhouette.
- Present this project in the form of a computer-designed booklet and also a talk to the whole family.

All my brothers had to do was to draw a chicken. And think of words to rhyme with each of five chicken words: *back, peck, chick, flock* and *cluck*. I asked what *back* had to do with chickens. "Nothing," said my dad, "but I wanted a word ending in the sound *ck*, and I need it to have *a* in it so I have each of the five vowels. It's called the *phonic method*." My brothers are quite advanced for four-year-olds. It's one of the annoying things about them.

Actually, I had already discovered that chickens are a lot more interesting than I'd thought. And by the time I'd finished my investigation, I was looking forward even more to the chickens coming.

These are some things I discovered:

1. One type of chicken, called the Araucana, lays blue eggs. This was not the type of chicken we were getting, unfortunately.
2. There are more chickens in the world than any other bird. About nine BILLION are born every year. That's a massive number.

It's much more than all the people in the world. Chickens could take over the universe if they were clever. Which, luckily, they are definitely not.

3. Wild chickens in the jungle lay about ten eggs a year. Chickens in a factory lay about 310. They must be exhausted.

4. When a chicken is in the mood for laying eggs, the comb on its head goes bright red.

5. If a chicken lays eggs with soft, bendy shells, you have to give it grit to eat.

6. Chickens have different personalities. Some have a sense of humour. I don't know how you tell when a chicken thinks something is funny, because as far as I could discover, they don't actually laugh, or even smile – well you couldn't with a beak, could you? – but that's what it said on the Internet. You are not supposed to believe everything you read on the Internet and I thought maybe that was one of those things.

I also discovered some things about hens that are kept in factories – battery hens. The things I discovered were extremely disgusting so I decided not to put them in my talk because my brothers are way too young to hear information like that. It's the sort of thing that could easily bring on projectile vomiting.

Anyway, with all that information, the project was not a problem and by tea-time I had finished off all the bits that I hadn't completed before. I had a slight headache, but I thought it was from all the hard work. After tea, I presented my talk. I decided to start with how to look after chickens. I felt that since the chickens were going to arrive the next day, the sooner my family understood everything about them the better. My dad did seem to have been reading a lot of books so he probably knew, but you can't be too careful with parents like mine. My mum had been building an ultrasonic electronic fox-detector but it wasn't quite finished. There are a lot of things in her new shed that are not quite finished.

They all sat round the kitchen table. I stood up. I don't know why I was nervous. After all, it was only my family. But I felt quite sort of shaky. A bit light-headed. As if my brain was on a stalk somewhere higher than it should be. I still had a headache.

I didn't know why. Not then.

Anyway, once they were all listening, I got started.

"Good evening, everyone," I began. I am quite

good at acting and I wanted to act the part of someone giving a lecture. I could be an actress actually. I probably will be. It could be another back-up job.

"Good evening," said my Harry Potter brother. The other one snorted.

"Boys!" said Dad crossly.

"Are you all right, Becca?" asked Mum.

"Yes, I'm fine," I said.

"Have you eaten properly?" asked Dad.

"Yes! Now can I please get on with this talk?"

"Boring!" said the other twin.

"Snoring!" said the Harry Potter one. They are obsessed with rhyming at the moment. I blame the *phonic method*.

"Boys! You listen to Becca or you'll do three hours' homework," said Dad, sounding as though he had been a teacher for ever. The twins looked at me, faces like angels. I carried on again. The dizziness increased. I felt hot and sweaty.

"I am going to talk to you about some important things to remember about looking after chickens. First, you must remember that chickens need lots of room to scratch around outside. They must have shelter from the sun, rain and wind. Also, make sure no foxes or anything can get in. It is a very good idea to have some grass and other plants growing. This encourages lots of things like insects and slugs, which the chickens like to eat."

"Eugggggghhhhhhh!" said both my brothers at the same time. Normally people say "eugggggghhh-hhhh" when they think something is disgusting. Not my brothers. It is a well-known fact that they like insects and slugs. All small boys do. They are weird. I remember a teacher in primary school telling us something once, which kind of explained it, I thought. He said that thousands of years ago, when humans lived in caves and things and were called *primitive*, they HAD to eat insects and slugs because sometimes there wasn't anything else. When he said that, I wondered if maybe small boys today still like insects and slugs because they are obviously very primitive and sort of closer to cave people than normal humans, especially girls. It makes sense.

"Shhh, boys. Listen to Becca," said Mum.

Then I forgot what I was going to say and I fainted. It only lasted a few seconds and I didn't actually completely faint. But I was aware of a crashing noise in my head, like rushing water in my ears, and everything went black and spinny.

I could hear voices around me and I heard Mum say, "Drink this, Becca." I felt the cup against my lips and I knew what it would be. Lucozade. And then I heard, "Eat this, Becca." And I felt something on my lips, which I guessed would be chocolate. It was. I ate a piece. I opened my eyes. I wished I hadn't. It was one of my brothers, with his face only about two inches from mine, holding the chocolate in his dirty hand and saying, "Eat this, Becca." The thought of projectile vomiting came into my mind. I closed my eyes again.

I knew what was going on. It's something that happens sometimes. I'll tell you why in a minute. But the weird thing was that normally the sweet drink and the chocolate makes me feel better straightaway. This time, oddly, I felt worse. I felt awful. My head felt hot and the black water was still rushing around my ears. I just wanted to go to bed.

I felt a tiny sting in my finger. I knew what that was. Then my mum said, "That's odd. Her blood sugar's normal."

"Not a hypo then," said Dad's voice. I was glad it wasn't.

Hypo is short for hypoglycaemia, which is what happens sometimes when you have diabetes. There. I've said it. And the sting in my finger was the blood-glucose-testing thing. It takes a tiny speck of blood and you put the blood on a strip of blue paper and you put the paper in a little machine and it tells you if your blood is OK. If it's not, you have to eat something sugary quickly and then it goes back to normal and you feel fine.

Maybe you have a headache, but that's all. It's really no big deal. As long as you've always got something sugary handy just in case. The only problem is you are supposed to tell people – your friends and everyone – in case you have a hypo when you are with them. So they will know what to do.

I just don't like telling people. Because the whole thing is no big deal. And I always end up having to tell them about the injections too. Then they always want to see. And they ALWAYS say, "Does it hurt?" So, just to save you from asking, I'll tell you, "No, it doesn't hurt. It's just boring, like always having to clean your teeth twice a day for the rest of your life."

Once, in the last year of primary school, when I'd only just started having diabetes, we happened to have a talk from the police about drugs. It was about how if we found a needle lying around outside we should not pick it up and we should just tell someone about it because it might be from a drug addict and it might have a disease like Aids on it. And one boy asked if you could catch Aids from someone with diabetes. Some people looked at me. Worried or embarrassed, I couldn't tell. After that, a group of girls started making signs of the cross when they passed me and calling me "druggy".

Stella and my other friends told our teacher. The next day I saw those girls walking out of the head's office. At least one of them had red eyes. I admit I was really pleased she had red eyes. She looked exceptionally ugly with red eyes. A bit like a very ill pig. The day after that, I got a letter from them saying sorry and that they hadn't understood. Personally, I don't think the letter was their idea. But they never did any of that stuff again. Pretty soon people just forgot about it, once they saw that I was actually just normal like everyone else. I mean, you don't tell someone with an asthma inhaler they're a drug addict, do you? So what's the difference? Grow up, I'd say if you did something like that.

I wasn't going to tell Jazz and Mel, or any other new friends I might make, about the diabetes. I decided.

Anyway, back to me feeling ill. But NOT having a hypo, according to the blood-testing thing.

Mum put her hand on my forehead. "She's hot as anything," she said. How hot is that, I wondered? "Must be a virus. Flu or something. Straight to bed, Becca." And that was it, straight to bed.

"But you don't know about chickens!" I mumbled, as I went upstairs with Mum.

She laughed. "Don't be silly. Of course I know about chickens. They have beaks and lay eggs and taste nice stuffed and roasted." My head felt as though something heavy was sitting on it and something thick and warm like hot potato soup was inside it, but I was very worried about those chickens. What if I was still ill the next day and they arrived without anyone sensible like me to be in charge?

"Don't forget the louse powder!" I called down the stairs.

"What's louse?" asked Bee— one of my brothers.

I didn't hear the answer but I did hear both my brothers screech "euuugggghhhhh", so they must have liked it.

As I climbed into my bed and Mum fussed around with the curtains and a glass of water and blood-glucose-testing strips and pushed all my clothes under the bed with her foot and took my temperature and found some paracetamol and did about a million things all at the same time, which is something she is amazingly good at, my brain was dividing itself into two halves, thinking two different things. One half was thinking how ill it felt and how it just wanted to sink into the pillow, pull the duvet up and go to sleep for about two weeks. The other half was worrying about those poor chickens arriving in our house and not having any responsible human to look after them. They would need me, those chickens would.

But there was another bad thought that crept into my head when I thought about the chickens. I had read somewhere that when chickens hatch, they remember the first face they see and become the best of friends with that face, whether it is a chicken or a human. It's called *imprinting*. I knew our chickens were not going to be babies, but wouldn't they end up liking everyone else in my family more than me if I wasn't around when they arrived? They might even *imprint* one of my brothers. Which would be seriously bad news for the chickens.

At this rate, I wasn't even going to have a chicken as my friend. I know I had Jazz and Mel, but what about when they were not there? I would need the chickens to like me best. I know it sounds really pathetic, but when you're ill things like that get to you. I have to admit that my eyes felt hot and a few tears tried to squeeze out and my nose filled up. Mum stroked my forehead but she didn't know what I was thinking. I kept it to myself. There wasn't anyone I could tell.

Stella would have understood. But, of course, if Stella had been here, I wouldn't have needed to worry about friends and people and chickens liking me anyway.

I fell asleep feeling sorry for myself, wishing I was someone else, somewhere else.

Feeling Sorry

I was still ill the next day. Every time I lifted my head off the pillow, I felt like a sick elephant. Heavy and grey and groaning.

When I closed my eyes, my feet and hands felt enormous. Frighteningly huge. When I opened them, my eyes hurt. It was a no-win situation.

I am sorry to moan but it was hell being ill. And I wasn't even missing school because I didn't go to school. And no one would know I was ill so no one would phone to ask how I was or write me a card or give me lots of attention when I went back to school. I couldn't read or watch TV because my eyes hurt too much. I didn't feel like eating but I had to because of diabetes. You have to eat with diabetes. I did get to eat nice things, like ice cream, as long as I watched my blood-sugar level. But nothing really tastes any good when you're ill, so there's not much point in being allowed to eat ice cream. Much better to have it when you're well. But you wouldn't normally get ice cream in the middle of a Wednesday morning if you were well. What a world! It's not really designed for pleasure, is it? Everything's the wrong way round.

My advice to you is, eat as much ice cream as you can when you are well because when you are ill you won't want it.

The chickens arrived after lunch. I heard a van arriving, and my dad shouting for everyone to come, and my brothers screeching as they charged down the stairs. They were singing, if you can call it singing, "Chick, chick, chick, chick, chicken."

I had to get out of bed. My head spun when I stood up. I tottered over to the window. I could see a man getting out of the van and my brothers jumping up and down trying to see into the windows. They were nowhere near tall enough.

Then the man got back into the van and drove round behind the house with my whole family running after it. They all went out of sight. I wanted to be there.

For the next hour I had to listen to the sounds of shrieking from my brothers and squawking from the chickens and crowing from the cockerel and crashing in my head.

You are probably sick of me going on about

feeling ill so I am not going to talk about it any more.

I will just say that it was a bad day. The worst since we had moved. Easily.

Jazz and Mel didn't even call round. I tried to tell myself that they must be busy. Their parents had probably forced them to stay at home. But I knew it was also possible that they didn't *want* to come back. Maybe I was so boring, they had completely forgotten that I existed at all. Maybe if I did something interesting to my hair they would remember me. Maybe if I was a completely different person they would remember me.

I got back into bed and felt sorry for myself again.

Chicken Friend

Next morning I definitely felt better. I would just forget about the day before, I decided. Maybe Jazz and Mel would come today. Mum let me get dressed, once she'd made sure I'd done all the boring stuff – the blood-sugar test and the injection. And, of course, I had to eat breakfast even though my tongue was furry. You can't skip meals when you have diabetes. As long as you don't skip meals, you'll be fine. Today it was boiled eggs.

"Not chicken eggs," said the HP twin.

"Oh? What sort of eggs then? Elephant eggs? Cow eggs?" I asked snappily. I was in no mood for their silliness.

"No, shop eggs, silly willy," said the other one.

"Oh right, shop eggs," I said. Sometimes, you just go along with it. I was glad the eggs weren't from our chickens anyway. I wanted to be the first to collect one.

I went out there straight after breakfast. On my own. Carrying all the things I thought my family might have forgotten. Like louse powder. I could hear the clucking as soon as I went outside. I don't know why people call it clucking. It was a gentle sort of rattly noise. A gravelly rumbling sound. A chirruping gossiping mumble. None of those things really describes it. You need to keep chickens to understand.

As I walked towards them I tried to smile at them in a reassuring way, as though I was definitely going to be their best friend. I imagined myself like the plump farmer's wife in a series of books my brothers were given last Christmas. The first time my dad read one he got very cross in a spluttering sort of way and kept asking why she had to be called a farmer's wife. I couldn't see the problem but he kept banging on about how people always assumed the man was the farmer and that the woman had to be called the farmer's wife. "Why couldn't she be the farmer and then her husband could be called the farmer's husband?" he asked. And instead of finishing reading the story to my brothers, he stomped off and wrote his own story about a farmer's husband. It was called "The Farmer's Husband Wins a Cake-Making Competition". He sent it off to the BBC but they sent it back saying it was quite an interesting idea but not very appealing to children.

Which made my dad crosser. From then on, he refused to read that story to my brothers, saying that he was going to "stand united in solidarity with women all over the world".

Anyway, back to the plump farmer's wife that I was imagining myself being. Not that I was plump, but she happens to be plump and has pink cheeks and a gentle smile and her thick hair is always wound in a bun with bits escaping from it. She always stands in the middle of the farmyard wearing an apron, and scatters grain from a bag that is attached to her waist. She just stands there scattering and smiling, and the chickens cluck around her feet and peck at the grain. So I opened the gate and stood there with that same farmer's-wife smile. And I scattered some grain.

I had not reckoned with the cockerel. In those storybooks, he was not a factor. He just cock-a-doodle-dooed at four every morning but he never interfered with the farmer's wife's job of scattering grain. This one did.

He leapt off the tree stump, where he had been standing, and ran towards the chickens, pecking at them and herding them into the henhouse. They all trotted off obediently, pointing their toes like ballet dancers pretending to be chickens, not even looking at me to see whether I was a plump, smiling, grain-scattering farmer's wife or not. I could have been a fox for all they cared. Once they were safely in, the cockerel came out and leapt onto the tree stump again, and crowed and crowed. That's what they do. Forget cock-a-doodle-dooing. That's strictly for storybooks. This one just crowed. Like a cross between a crow and a trumpet. And he did not look me in the eye. He waved his flowing black tail feathers at me as though I should be impressed. Then he actually turned his back on me.

I was not going to be fazed by some cocky cockerel. I had, remember, read a lot about chickens. And I am a human being. Therefore I am superior.

I advanced confidently, with a handful of grain ready. I scattered some in front of him, which he pretended to ignore. I did see him look at it, though. He could not fool me – I knew the grain would be too much of a temptation for him. He turned his head, glanced at me out of one eye and then ... you probably won't believe me but I swear it's true ... he winked.

Once I had recovered from the shock, I decided this was a sign of friendship. He may not exactly have *imprinted* me but at least I was accepted. I turned my back on him and walked towards the henhouse. The cockerel leapt from his perch and raced ahead of me, still crowing as loudly as he could. He flapped onto the henhouse roof and stood there, puffing out all his feathers and crowing, as though he was saying, "Here comes a human – don't say I didn't warn you! But I'll just stay out here if you don't mind. Deal with it yourselves – I've done my bit."

As I walked in, this enormous sort of humming, crooning noise rose from the hens. There they all were, some on the ground and some in their nests, which were really boxes filled with straw on a shelf. They looked at me warily. I smiled at them. They maybe didn't understand smiling, not being able to do it themselves, what with their beaks, as I mentioned before. So I spoke gently to them, and tried to sound as little like a fox as possible.

There were nine birds altogether, ten including the cockerel. We were each allowed to choose names for two of them. The twins were warned not to choose something rude or disgusting. Mum and Dad had said I could choose my chickens first, since I had missed them when they arrived.

One particular chicken caught my eye. She was pecking around in a corner, picking up every last bit of grain or anything remotely like food. When she turned towards me I could see that the feathers under her neck were quite scraggy and I remembered why. All these chickens had been rescued from a battery farm and had been badly treated. The man who had rescued them had looked after them till they recovered but he did say that some of them still had scraggy feathers. I felt sorry for her, but I was glad she was here with us and not on a battery farm. Watching her cleaning up every last speck off the ground I decided she had to be called Cinderella.

There was a very white chicken with a bright red comb on her head. I decided she would be my other one, but I couldn't think of a name. I would have to see what sort of personality she had. She was sitting there on her nest, making rumbling noises in her throat. That did not particularly help with choosing a name.

I walked out of the shed and scattered some grain just outside the door. The chickens followed, muttering and chattering as they pecked the grain. I felt just like a farmer's wife after all. It was a very relaxing feeling. It almost made me not mind about Jazz and Mel not coming round yesterday or even if they didn't come today. Almost.

It made me think that living in the country might end up being fun after all.

I have a sneaking suspicion that all this obsessive chicken stuff is making me sound a bit boring again, but actually I don't care. I'm sorry, but I like chickens. I like being responsible for them. They are undemanding. They don't mind whether

I'm boring or not. Maybe we should all be a bit more like chickens. Then we wouldn't have to worry about things like world peace and drug problems and whether we are eating five portions of fruit a day.

I went over to check that they had fresh water and a bowl of grit. They did. My family had not done too badly. I was actually a bit annoyed that I hadn't found any disasters.

Just then the white hen come out of the hen-house and joined the others. I watched her peck at the grain. There was something very odd about the way she did it. She started close to her and pecked around in a neat and precise circle, which got wider and wider until there was a completely clear space around her. How tidy! How organized! And I knew immediately what she should be called. I knew only one person who was as tidy and organized as that. Stella! Well, and Stella's mum obviously, but I couldn't call a chicken "Stella's mum", could I?

"Stella!" I called. "Come here, Stella." I would like to be able to tell you that she turned round and looked at me. That's what she would have done if this had been a story. But, of course, she didn't. She was still definitely Stella, though.

I went into the empty henhouse to put some louse powder on the nests. And that was when

I found it! Our first egg! My first egg! And, of course, it was Stella who had laid it. It was her present to me.

At least I had a chicken friend.

The Inspector

The next morning, a woman from the education department came round. To inspect us, my dad said. The people in London must have told the people in the West Country about us. There was no escape. My dad was delighted, though. He kept rubbing his hands in pleasure at the thought of showing this inspector just how well he and Mum were doing.

Her name was Mrs Gordon. My dad called her Mrs Gorgon. A gorgon is a very ugly woman with snakes for hair. Mrs Gordon wasn't that ugly but my dad still called her that. The first time he did it, she said, quite firmly, "It's *Gordon*, Mrs Gordon."

"That's what I said," said Dad, looking at her directly. I practically believed him myself. He carried on calling her Mrs Gorgon, but in such a cleverly mumbling way that she could never be quite sure whether he was saying Gordon or Gorgon.

Dad made her a cup of herbal tea in the kitchen. I think she probably wanted coffee instead of herbal tea but my dad just said, "Shall I make you a cup of herbal tea, Mrs Gorgon?" and she couldn't really say, "No, I'd rather have coffee," could she?

My dad quickly swept a curled-up slice of courgette off the chair that Mrs Gorgon was about to sit on. Then, in one really smooth movement, he also very quickly closed the blind on the window just near her that looked into the garden. "Sun's awfully bright today," he said with a smile, even though it actually wasn't. But I knew why he'd closed the blind. Mum was outside her shed trying out her new anti-fly hat, which looked something like a helicopter on the top of her head. We called it her heli-hat. She also had a large plaster on her forehead from when she had hit her head, again, on the brain-drain chair. She had taken a break from the brain-drain chair. She said it needed some *modification*. Dad said it needed binning.

Sometimes he's proud of my mum. Sometimes he's not. Usually it depends on whether she has just damaged something or ended up in hospital. Once he said that being married to her was like being a single father with four children. He said he would have liked to write about her in a story but he hadn't because no one would believe the story.

Thank goodness. There's only one thing I can think of more embarrassing than having a father who writes tacky TV programmes and a mother who invents useless things, and that's a father who writes a tacky TV programme ABOUT a mother who invents useless things. That would be called a double whammy.

"So, Mrs Gorgon? What can we do for you? Biscuit? The twins made them." Dad offered her a plate.

"How nice. And how clever!" said Mrs Gorgon, smiling at the twins, who happened to walk through the kitchen at that moment. "What did you make them with?"

"Dog poo!" said the Harry Potter one.

Are all brothers as embarrassing and disgusting as mine? The twins are obsessed with dog poo just now. Well, not the actual dog poo itself, just the word. When it's just us in the house they don't usually bother about it, but you can bet that as soon as someone like Great-aunt Margie or Mrs Gordon comes round, or any time they are supposed to behave properly, they'll be saying everything is dog poo. Next month it might be something else. Luckily, they won't be going to school so they won't learn about Personal and Social Education, otherwise they would definitely learn words that would be even more embarrassing.

The twins each grabbed a biscuit and went outside. My dad shut the door behind them.

"You should have something to eat, Becca," he said, looking at his watch.

"I just had something," I lied. It was only a small lie. I didn't want to talk about it in front of Mrs Gordon. I don't like telling total strangers why I have to eat things in the middle of the morning. I would have something soon, when Mrs Gordon had gone.

I smiled at Mrs Gordon. I think I realized that she was the one who could make us go back to school if she decided that my mum and dad couldn't teach us. Personally, I wouldn't have minded about school, but I did NOT want Mrs Gordon thinking Mum and Dad were useless. Even if they were. There are some things families should keep secret. "The biscuits are nice, really," I said. "My brothers just say silly things. They did make them, though. We often do the cooking. Mum forgets and dad's a writer."

I twiddled my New York apple earrings.

Mrs Gordon didn't eat a biscuit.

She sort of shifted herself onto the edge of the chair and sat with her ankles crossed. She was wearing quite high heels. She wouldn't be able to walk far in those. And I thought her skirt was a bit short, for someone as old as her. She must have been at least middle-aged, maybe even forty. Luckily, she didn't put her elbows on the table. There is usually something old and sticky on our kitchen table.

"Now, Mr Jarrett, perhaps we could have a little talk."

"Certainly, Mrs Gorgon. Fire away."

She looked at me. She tried to smile, but in a stern, grown-up way. "Perhaps, um, Rebecca, isn't it?"

"Becca," I said, feeling what my dad would call a *situation* coming on. But when I sneaked a look at him, he was just smiling. He looked as though nothing was going to bother him that day.

"Yes, well, perhaps your father and I could have a little talk together? And is your mother here? Perhaps I could talk to her as well?"

"I'm so sorry, Mrs Gordon, but Jill is *very* busy at the moment," said my dad loudly, trying to drown the sudden shouting from outside. I twisted my head till I could just see through another window that the not-Harry Potter twin was now wearing Mum's heli-hat and the Harry Potter one was shouting "My turn! My turn!" and tugging at Mum's clothes. Mum had a cordless screwdriver in one hand, the ear of the twin who was wearing the hat in the other hand (because she needed him to stand still while she screwed something on the heli-hat, I suppose) and a shortbread biscuit in her mouth – she always eats shortbread when she needs to concentrate. Then I saw the Harry Potter one let go of her and go towards the garden hose. It didn't take a genius to know what he was going to do. I pushed my chair back very quickly and rushed to the door, shouting, "Dad, one of the rabbits is out." We don't have any rabbits but he knew what I meant.

Shutting the door behind me I ran down the garden and grabbed both the twins and said to them in a fierce voice, "That lady in there. Do you know who she is?"

"No," they both nodded together. I think I forgot to tell you. That's what they do. They nod when they say no and they shake their heads when they say yes. I don't know how they do it. I tried once. It's even harder than patting your head with one hand while making your hand go round and round on your stomach.

Mum had now taken the heli-hat and the twins hadn't even noticed. That's how much power I have when I get really angry.

"She's the chief police person of the whole country. And she wants to make you go back to nursery. And if she thinks you are naughty or wild or go around making dog-poo biscuits, she *will* make you go to nursery. Today!"

"Mum gived our nursery sweatshirts to cancer," said one, looking pleased with himself.

"It wouldn't matter," I hissed. "She'd make you go in your pyjamas. And it's *gave*."

"Mum gived my 'jamas to cancer," said the other, looking extremely pleased with himself.

"*Gave*. No, she didn't. She *bought* your pyjamas from cancer – from the cancer charity shop, I mean. Anyway, that's not the point. That lady in there can make you go to school. We have to show her that Mum and Dad can teach us everything."

"Sugar!" shouted Mum. She had not been listening to this conversation. She had put the heli-hat on her own head to make another adjustment to it, but this had made the heli bit of it fly into the air and land in some bushes.

"Go on, boys," said Mum. "Who can find it first?" And they dived into the bushes. There was a lot of shrieking and branches that looked as though they had lives of their own. Mum, still wearing the hat, scrabbled around on the grass trying to find any other small bits that were missing.

Something made me glance back at the house. Just as the door was opening and Dad and Mrs Gordon were coming out. "Mum!" I said, urgently. "Mum! Get up!"

She looked up. "Oh, hello!" she said, standing

up and managing to speak with three small screws held between her teeth. Goodness knows where the shortbread was. She walked towards Mrs Gordon and Dad. Still wearing the hat.

Things were not going well at all. I ran over to the boys and pulled them out of the bushes. "Boys, listen, *that's* the chief police person there. She has come to see you," I muttered to them. "You must be *very* quiet and polite. Say hello very nicely. But don't shake her hand," I warned, looking at their hands. I didn't really need to look. I think you can imagine what they were like.

We walked towards Mrs Gordon and the twins did *exactly* what I had said. At first. Then the Harry Potter one had to take things a little bit too far. He bowed to Mrs Gordon. He actually *bowed*. I mean *where* did he get that from? Must be TV or something. I seem to remember they watched *Little Lord Fauntleroy* last Christmas. Anyway, Mrs Gordon looked at him as though he was a toad or something nasty that had got on her shoe.

"Hello," said the twin who bowed. "I don't go to school. I'm a twin." He wrinkled his nose to straighten his specs.

"How do you do?" said Mrs Gordon. "I'm very pleased to meet you." And she held out her hand. I didn't even have time to think, let alone do anything.

"Becca said don't shake your hand," he said.

"Oh!" said Mrs Gordon. By this time, her face had gone red. Angry red. Not the sort of hot and confused red you go when you've been on my mum's brain-drain chair and the one-minute timer has gone wrong. Things were becoming uncomfortable. I had the feeling that I was on a go-cart that was going out of control down a hill that was getting steeper every second.

"It's just their hands, Mrs Gorgon," I said. "We were just going to wash them."

And it was only as I heard the strangled sort of splutter from Dad that I realized. I had called her Mrs Gorgon. Clear as water.

Amazingly, Mrs Gordon must have written a report that said Mum and Dad could teach us, because we got a letter a week later. I think perhaps she was friends with the teachers in a local primary school and could not bring herself to let my brothers loose on them.

Robin's Revenge

Jazz and Mel came at lunchtime that day. When I saw them coming through the gate, I was excited and nervous at the same time. They said they had an afternoon off. Mel had eye make-up on and her lip-gloss glistened stickily. I hadn't had time to put any on. Though I was wearing my crocodile-eating-its-own-tail earrings.

Now, of course, I realize they probably didn't have an afternoon off. Unless you call bunking off school after lunchtime register an afternoon off. But then, I believed everything they said. I was just pleased they had chosen to spend their time with me. "Come with us," said Jazz. "We're going into the village." Mel wiped the screen of her mobile phone.

"I don't know. I've got ... stuff to do. I'm probably not allowed."

Mel did this thing with her mouth. One corner

went up so that one side of her nose wrinkled towards her eye, and her chin went down and her head shook slowly from side to side as though she could hardly bring herself to believe she was talking to someone as boring as me. I don't blame her. I sounded pathetic.

"So, make something up or just say you'll be back soon or, I don't know, just say *something*. Come on, Becks, we want you to come. It'll be cool."

"It'll be fun," said Jazz. "We'll show you where everyone lives and that. You need to get out and about. You can meet the gang. There are some boys. They'll like you. We'll text them." Mel started texting.

"Yeah, cool," I said. What else could I say? "I'll just ask my mum."

"Just *tell* your mum," said Mel scornfully. "Thought your olds were supposed to be mega-cool."

Just then I heard my mum shouting from her shed. Loudly. Very loudly. "Help! Becca! Help!"

I couldn't believe the timing of it. I mean what do you *do* when you're eleven years old and your mum shouts for you and these two girls who you are desperate to impress are wanting you to go with them? I could feel the blood rushing to my face. I could feel the panic in my stomach.

"Oh, whatever," said Mel. "We can see you've got major probs here." She did that mouth thing again and closed her phone cover – without sending the text, I think.

"Look, come back tomorrow, OK? It'd be great. Really great."

"Hey, how about we bring some of the gang round?" said Mel suddenly, her eyes flicking around. "I mean, you've got a cool place here. There's room for, I don't know, *anything*."

"Yeah, sure," I said. "Anything."

I should never have said that. It was my mum's fault.

No, it probably wasn't my mum's fault really. I don't want to think about it.

Anyway, of course, I ran to help Mum. I know that voice. It means there's a problem. "Come back tomorrow," I shouted as I ran. "It'd be cool. Really cool."

"Becca! Someone! Quick!" Last time my mum shrieked like that she was being pinned against a wall by the robot she was working on. It had rebelled.

Some things never change. Some things you want to change. Others you don't. Frankly, I was getting fed up with running to help my mum every time she had a problem. And it was worse now I didn't go to school. I seemed to be on duty all the time. It was as though there was no escape.

Feeling prickly with anger, I opened the door to her shed. She was, again, being bullied by the robot. I haven't told you about the robot before. To be honest, I didn't think you'd believe me. I may have given you the idea that my mum is truly hopeless at inventing. Actually, she has about three university degrees in robotics. She can make robots that do almost anything. Well, not usually anything very useful, but anything else. If she could channel her energies into something useful, it might be worth having a mother who was an inventor. She could even be famous and we could be rich.

Right then she was working on a robotic bin. She still is, actually – it never got finished, what with everything. It's called the Robin. Short for robot-bin, if you hadn't got that. The idea was that it would follow its owner round so that the owner could just put rubbish in it at any moment without having to get up and go to the bin. She wants my brothers to have one each. She thinks parents all over the world will think this is a brilliant idea and will want to buy their children one. She plans to make a fortune. It is probably the best idea she has ever had. I think my brothers might even like it, though they would probably put disgusting things in it.

Unfortunately, if you try to make a robot do something too complicated, it can go crazy. It's a bit like having a nervous breakdown for robots. Robots are not like other machines at all. Did you know that they can actually learn new behaviour which the inventor maybe didn't even intend? It's truly amazing. When I think how clever you'd have to be to make something like that, I almost have to respect my mum. Almost. I just WISH she would leave me out of it. Unless she would pay me to be her assistant. That would be OK. Then I would have rights.

Anyway, she had managed to make the Robin follow a person. But she hadn't managed to make it stop before knocking the person over. Or at least pushing itself against the person. I saw a dog do that to an old lady's leg once. The old lady was not happy about it at all. She used her stick in quite a violent way. Which made me wonder why she needed the stick for walking at all if she was strong enough to be so violent. Or maybe she frequently got attacked by dogs like this and took the stick as a sensible precaution.

When I say "knocking the person over", I am actually exaggerating. But at this moment the robot was whirring loudly as it bashed itself again and again against Mum. Now, normally she would have been able to deal with this. After all, the robot was much smaller than her. However, there was a problem. It was the brain-drain chair again. I wish she would drop that idea. It will never catch on. Anyway, she was still working on it. *In* it, in fact. And, yes, she was upside down and, yes, the one-minute timer had broken again. She had grabbed hold of the wrong remote control and had accidentally switched *on* the Robin instead of switching *off* the brain-drain chair. Meanwhile, the remote control for the chair had fallen out of her pocket and she was now stuck upside down with the Robin bashing against her head.

I almost forgot how cross I was. I mean, I had to laugh.

In order to understand properly the funny side of this situation, you need to know what the Robin looked like. If you are thinking of robins, think again. It was designed especially for one of my brothers, so it was built to look like his favourite football star. My mum's idea was that the football player's head flipped open, revealing ABSOLUTELY nothing inside, and my brother would put his rubbish in and then the head would flip closed again and a voice would shout "Goal!" So, my mum was actually being attacked by a miniature football player shouting, "Goal!" at her over and over again, while kicking her on the side of the head. Because she was upside down, you'll remember.

There was no time to find the correct remote control. (Usually there are at least twenty-five hanging around.) Besides, I prefer to use my own arms for simple tasks. There is less chance of things going wrong. So I just picked up the football player and put him face down, trapped in the corner, where he continued to shout, "Goal!" in a muffled way while his head flipped open and shut, and his little legs twitched. I swung the chair upright and helped Mum out. She looked a bit red, but more pleased with herself than she should have done.

"I really think I'm getting somewhere with that!" she said happily. "Thanks, Becca."

I could have said, "No problem," but that wouldn't have been true. "Mum?"

"Mmmm?" she said, absent-mindedly as she opened up one of the remote controls.

"There're two girls, Jazz and Mel, and they're going to come round tomorrow." Silence. The Robin stopped shouting, "Goal!" and lay still. I continued. "And I was wondering if, well…" I stopped. I tried to think of a slightly more tactful way of saying, "Could you all please stay about a million miles away so that you don't completely embarrass me and put my new friends off for life, not to mention making us the laughing stock of the village? Especially my brothers?" But I couldn't quite think of a way to say it that would get the desired effect. Anyway, was she listening? It didn't look like it, as she fiddled with tiny tools inside the remote control.

"Mum, are you listening?"

"Mmm? Ah! That's it!"

"Mum! You didn't hear a word I said, did you!"

"Yes, I did. You said there are two girls, Jel and Mazz, or something modern, and they're going to come round tomorrow. And you were wondering if, well… What were you wondering? I expect you were wondering if your family could stay about a million miles away so that we don't embarrass you and put your new friends off for life, and make us the laughing stock of the village? Especially your brothers."

Sometimes, parents can REALLY surprise you.

"Well, yes, I was, actually."

"No problem. I'll get the boys to make some biscuits and then we'll just—"

"No! No biscuits! Please!"

"Only joking," she said. "Now, would you please pass the doobry?"

"Which one?"

"The one with the thingy at the end of it."

I passed her the doobry with the thingy at the end of it and left the shed.

"Thanks, Becca," said Mum as I went. "And I'm glad you've found some new friends. I knew you would."

I went to see Stella and Cinderella on the way back to the house. The sun was lasering down and making my hair smell of fresh pancakes. The chickens were clucking contentedly. The cockerel – which, by the way, the twins have called Cocky, with a typical lack of imagination – was strutting up and down like a soldier. There was a heat haze wobbling over the faraway hills. And I could hear the water trickling in the brook that gave our house its name.

It's going to be all right, I thought to myself. It really is.

It really wasn't.

Party Plan

Jazz and Mel came the next day. Without "the gang", luckily. This time I was prepared. I spent pretty much most of the morning getting ready (apart from the bit where I rushed through my work). Getting ready involved taking everything out of my wardrobe and putting each thing on and looking at myself in the mirror, trying to imagine I was Mel looking at me. I had a black top I thought would do. It wasn't completely black but there was definitely more black than anything else. It was a bit hot for the summer but I couldn't help that. I rooted around among my nail varnishes and managed to find a blue one that wasn't too ancient and congealed. Earrings – well, lots of choices there, of course. I picked some in the shape of Manolo Blahnik shoes.

I made my hair messy. That was easy. And jeans. It had to be the same ones as before, unfortunately.

They probably could have been a bit more fashionable. I'd never really looked at them through Mel's eyes before. Suddenly, I looked so totally uncool. I even thought I was maybe a bit fat. I'd NEVER thought that before. My face had cheeks instead of hollows like Mel's. I sucked them in a bit, but that never really works because then as soon as you speak the air goes in and puffs them out again.

You probably think I'm a real saddo. Yes, so I'd lived in London. You'd think a city girl moving to the country would have the advantage in the fashion-coolness stakes. But Stella and I and our other friends were never that bothered. Somehow, Mel and Jazz seemed to make more of an effort with clothes and stuff than ANYONE I knew in London. We were always too busy just doing things and having fun. I mean, it's not that I'm unfashionable, honestly, but you need to understand that there are degrees of fashionableness these days, and on a scale of one to ten, I was definitely somewhere around five. Well, I would be, wouldn't I? In the middle. Average. Miss Boring.

Well, I'd go shopping soon. Maybe with Jazz and Mel? That would be great.

When I saw them coming through our gate, my stomach lurched. I quickly stuffed all the papers from my desk into a drawer, hid the book I was reading, pushed all my clothes into my cupboard, hid my injection kit and everything under my bed as well, put my head upside down so my hair would go messier, and scowled at myself in the mirror. Oh, and then I took the photo of Stella off my bedside table and put it gently face down in a drawer. Sorry, Stella. It was only for your protection.

"They're here, Mum!" I called as I slid down the banisters. Dad was out, and Mum had promised that as soon as Jazz and Mel arrived she would take the boys to the shops in the car. As long as I promised to get my maths done. Easy. I'd have revised for five physics tests and learnt all the French verbs in existence to get my brothers out of the way. Temporarily, I mean.

I could hear her in the kitchen. To be fair to her, she was doing her best to hurry the boys out of the back door. But they were not co-operating. One of them wanted a drink and the other said he was hungry, and then the one who wanted a drink said he needed the toilet, and the one who was hungry spilt the other one's drink. Sometimes things like this make me just laugh. Other times, I feel so angry that this scream starts to brew inside me, and rise and rise through my stomach and up to my throat, and it SO wants to come out that one day I think it might. Then everyone would be shocked because I am not supposed to be a screaming sort of person. Anyway, just then was definitely a needing-to-scream time. It grated through me like gravel between my teeth.

"I'll do it, Mum." I said, grabbing a cloth and mopping frantically. The doorbell rang and I rushed through to get it, shouting, "Bye," to my mum. I opened the door and tried to get Mel and Jazz to come quickly up the stairs but it was no good. There were the twins in the kitchen doorway and there was my mum in the hall.

"Hello, girls, nice to see you again," she said. Both the twins were staring at Mel and Jazz. They can do truly evil stares when they want to. It's all an act. But when they do it, you can easily imagine them starring in a horror film as the possessed children of the devil. Then B— one of them did his new about-to-be-sick face where his mouth opens and his throat contracts and his stomach heaves like waves, and you really do think he is about to throw up. He even makes the retching noise to go with it.

"Mum..." I said. "Um, weren't you...?"

"Yes, darling, I just need to get a clean jumper for L—" I had a sudden, very loud coughing fit.

"Let's go outside and see the chickens," I said, recovering quickly. And I almost pushed Mel and Jazz out of the house. "Families!" I said with a scowl, as I led them round the side of the house.

98

"What a nightmare!"

"Chickens?" asked Mel, with her face just about to do that thing again. "How boring is that?" Then she started grinning. She turned to Jazz. "Hey, Jazz, maybe I should introduce Saddam to the chickens!"

"Yuck!" said Jazz. "You're gross, Mel!"

"Who's Saddam?" I asked.

"Mel's brother's python. Don't worry, she's only joking."

I didn't think I wanted to show them the chickens any more. "OK, what shall we do?" I asked, stopping. I fingered my Manolo Blahnik earrings. They didn't notice.

"Chickens," said Mel. "I want to see the chickens. I want to see Saddam's tea." Then she looked at me and saw my face, probably with my eyes all screwed up and tense. "Just a joke, Becks. Don't take things so seriously."

"No, really," and I grinned with a huge effort because grinning was absolutely the last thing my face wanted to do. "I was just thinking of something else."

"Oh right! Like I believe you! So, what were you thinking of then?" Her face was split in a huge grin. She linked arms with Jazz. "We've got to cheer her up, Jazzy. It's our duty as her friends, don't you think?"

"My gross brothers," I said at last. "That's all

I was thinking about." It was all I could think of.

"No!" exclaimed Mel and unlinked her arms from Jazz and put her hands over her ears. "Don't talk to me about those grossnesses. Don't pollute your head with thoughts of them! It's majorly bad for you. You've got to learn to chill, Becks!" I didn't like the *Becks* thing particularly but it was only because she was being nice to me, I thought. It's what you do when you're friends with someone. It should make me feel great that she wanted to have a special name for me. It did really.

"Can we see the chickens?" asked Jazz. "It'd be cool."

I looked at Mel. She grinned. "OK, chickies, here we come," she said. "Lead on, Becks." She linked arms with me and Jazz, one on each side of her. My mum's car drove past us as we went, with my brothers both sticking their tongues out and one of them licking the window, looking straight at Jazz and Mel. Mel stuck one finger up at them. I hoped my mum hadn't seen.

The chickens were strutting around pecking at this and that. The cockerel was standing on his tree-stump with one eye shut and his head to one side. He opened the other eye then ruffled up his black feathers like a cloak, and crowed as though to say, "Don't think I haven't seen you, but actually I can't be bothered to jump down off here just now, it being a rather hot day. But I am watching you, so just don't try anything."

"Cock-a-doodle-doo to you," said Jazz. "Can we feed them, Becca?"

There's a little store shed just outside the chicken run, where we keep the food and grit and stuff, so I gave her a scoop of seed and showed her how to scatter it. She started scattering. "Cool!" she shouted as the chickens started pecking nearby. "Come on, Mel, come and feed the little chickies."

Mel stepped carefully through the gate, holding up the bottoms of her jeans (but still with her phone in her hand as usual) and screwing up her face in disgust. Jazz passed her the scoop of grain and Mel let go of one trouser leg and dipped her fingers in and sprinkled some seed. But she sprinkled it so close to her feet that the chickens came crowding round her and she lifted her feet high trying to step away from them. She must have accidentally stepped on a chicken's foot because it leapt up with a squawk. The cockerel started crowing and leapt off his perch and came charging towards her with his neck out-stretched and his eyes blazing madly. Mel threw the whole scoop in the air and ran. I opened the gate for her and she charged through screaming, arms flapping.

She didn't see me laughing, luckily. She only saw Jazz doubled over in spasms of hysterics.

"Shut up, you cow!" she shouted at Jazz. "That bloody hen-thing attacked me! I could have dropped my phone!" Her face was red and her lips were quivering. I almost thought she was going to cry. This was a disaster. Maybe quite a funny disaster but definitely a disaster. I could not have Mel crying. I needed her to have a great afternoon at my house so that she would think I was a cool friend.

"It's a cockerel, not a hen," said Jazz, still laughing.

"That happened to me the first time I went in," I lied to Mel. "I don't blame you." Mel said nothing but her lips looked a bit stronger. "What do you want to do?" I asked her. "We could go and get something to eat and take it to this special place I've got."

"Yeah, whadever," she replied.

"Come on, Jazz," I said. I didn't want her to be left out. I knew instinctively that I did not want the two of them arguing. I wanted us all to be friends together. People say "three's a crowd" but I don't see why it should be like that.

This time, I linked one arm into Jazz's and one into Mel's and I guided them towards the house. This feeling built up inside me – a buttery, warm, yellow FANTASTIC feeling. I was in the middle, not on the edge.

They seemed impressed by the choice of food we had in our kitchen. We have a huge tin, seriously huge, with loads of chocolate bars as well as low-sugar snacks for me. I have to be careful not to have too much sugar. And there's another huge tin with home-made biscuits and flapjacks and things in. Of course, I didn't mention that the twins had made some of them. And Mum had made an amazing gooey chocolate cake – low-sugar, obviously – which she'd left out for us. Every now and then she does get her act together and do proper mother things. The things you read about mothers doing in books. Actually, I hate those books – after all, anyone can make a cake, but not everyone's mother has three degrees in robotics. I'm not complaining about the cake, though. The perfect situation would be a mother who made great cakes when your friends came round AND had three degrees in robot science. And then stayed completely out of the way.

So, we took some food and drinks, and I led them out to the barn. It's not really a barn. It's called a linny, which is like a small barn but only has three walls. One of the long sides is open. You use it to store bales of hay or farm equipment, or whatever, but we don't have any. All the garden furniture is in there, plus some old straw bales because the people who were here before us kept a pony.

The view is amazing from the linny, over miles of fields and rolling hills that look like a whole flock of sleeping hippopotamuses, except they're green and yellow. In some fields there are cows just doing nothing. From time to time you see a tractor going backwards and forwards making patterns in the yellow stuff that grows there. And there's the stream trickling past, not far from the linny, part of the way along the edge of our land. It's mostly very shallow, but there's one deeper bit further down. My brothers were told never to go near, not even the shallow bit but especially not the deep bit, not until my dad had finished making a wire fence. My parents are actually quite sensible about important things like that.

Outside the linny my dad had started building a barbecue that was going to be amazing – huge, big enough for about twenty burgers at a time. He said we could have a barbecue on my birthday.

"I use this as my hideaway," I said, as we approached. "I haven't done much to it yet, but maybe you can help. My brothers aren't allowed here on their own, because of the stream," I explained.

"Cool!" said Jazz.

"Most cool!" said Mel. She was looking all around. "We could have a party here! We could have such a cool party!"

"Actually, it's my birthday next week and I was going to—"

"Most cool," repeated Mel, suddenly smiling in a very friendly way. "That would be so cool. Most definitely. We could help you and you probably don't know many people so we could bring some friends for you. We could have music and we could do stuff," she continued, getting all excited. "Couldn't we, Jazzy?"

"And food and drink – we could help you choose, Becca," said Jazz.

"We could ask Joe and Sharky and Corally and—"

"And Sophie," said Jazz. "*If* we've forgiven her by then, of course."

"Why? What did she do?" I asked

"Do? What didn't the little tart do?" said Mel.

Jazz explained. "Mel was going out with Sharky and Sophie was going out with Joe, or she was *supposed* to be but Corally said she saw Sophie kissing Sharky in the shopping centre even though Sophie said she'd never been there that day but then Sassy said she'd seen Sophie there too but this time with Paulo and even though they were only walking around Sassy swears they were almost

105

holding hands and Paulo is supposed to be going out with Dee so *whatever* Sophie was doing that day she was being a tart."

"What a cow!" I said. I don't know why that came out. Frankly I couldn't care one way or the other about all these people, but I was starting to feel that if I didn't say something to get in on the action, then I'd be left severely outside. Mel nodded in approval at my good judgement.

"Most cowish," agreed Jazz.

"A bitch," I said.

"Bitchier," said Jazz.

"Most bitchy!" Mel added, grinning.

"But you might forgive her," I said, remembering just in time. I didn't want to be on record as having said anything bad about this Sophie if Sophie was going to be one of the guests at my birthday party. I do know you have to be careful about these things. I have had friends before, remember.

"If she's lucky," said Mel.

"OK, so this party," said Jazz. "When's it going to be?"

"Maybe not on her actual birthday," said Mel.

"Why not?" I asked.

"Cos your family might get involved," said Jazz. "They might want to come, of course, which would be a major disaster. Though your family's a bit weird – maybe they wouldn't come?"

"We had a Jehovah's Witness kid at school once and it's against their religion to have birthdays. Maybe your parents are like that," said Mel, adjusting her top so that it was just off her shoulders. She had to stretch the neck to do that, which my mum would say was a bit silly because it wouldn't shrink back again. I almost agree. Though it did look quite kind of sexy.

We were not Jehovah's Witnesses and we certainly celebrated birthdays. But that made me think, yes, of course my family would want to be at my birthday party and of course I wanted my family at my birthday party but ... maybe not at this particular birthday party. Mel was right, it would have to be a different day from my birthday. Twin four-year-old brothers, a father who writes tacky kids' TV programmes, a mother with a tendency to hang upside down and some cool new friends just don't come together in a chapter called, "A Wonderful Birthday Party".

Anyway, we got it all sorted. We spent the next hour lying on our backs on the grass outside the linny. We all pulled our trouser legs up so we could get the sun on our legs. Mel and Jazz had sunglasses but they didn't put them on because they said it would make a white mark. I wanted to wear mine because my eyes always get watery and squinty in the sun, but I didn't want a white mark if they didn't want one, so we all just kept our eyes shut as we planned my party.

All I had to do was sort it with my mum and dad that evening after Mel and Jazz had gone. And I did. It was easy. Mum and Dad were really pleased that I had found some friends who wanted to have a party with me.

"I thought they looked fun, Becca," said Mum. "I loved the braidy things in Jel's hair."

"Jazz, Mum, that one's Jazz. Can I get some new clothes, please?"

And even that was sorted. Mum would take me into the shopping centre to get some new clothes for my birthday present. On my birthday we would have a family barbecue, and the day before that my new friends would come round, and we would be left to our own devices in the linny. They couldn't leave us completely alone in the house but they understood about keeping out of the way, so Mum would take the twins swimming and shopping and Dad promised to stay in his study all afternoon. I could pretend he wasn't there. (Secretly, I would tell my friends my parents were so cool that they had left us alone.) I could have whatever food I liked.

It sounded perfect.

Just before I went to sleep that night, I realized

I hadn't thought about Stella once since Mel and Jazz had arrived that day. I had even left her photo in my drawer. I was too tired to get out of bed and rescue it. I would do it in the morning.

But then I lay there and lay there and thought about Stella. I got up and took her photo from the drawer and put it back beside my bed. As I looked at it, the Stella time seemed strangely far away. I couldn't quite remember what her voice sounded like.

Never mind, I thought. I'll email her in the morning. Or phone her or something.

This would be the first party I could remember when Stella had not been there, making everyone laugh. You almost don't have to think of anything to say when Stella is there because she can always make a party be fun, just by being there. I hoped this party would be like that. It was really important that people liked me. But I wasn't good at thinking of things to say, like Stella. Wacky things. Funny things. Things that made you think of things to say yourself. Things that made everyone glad to be a friend of Stella's best friend.

But I have to say one thing. I am ashamed of it, I really am, especially now, but I was actually glad Stella wouldn't be there. I didn't know why then. I do now. It's because she would notice that I was different when I was with Jazz and Mel. And she would disapprove, even though she wouldn't have said anything. Stella always says you should be who you are and not pretend to be someone else. That's easy for Stella. Stella is Stella and everyone likes her that way. But me? When you look at Jazz and Mel, and then you look at me, who do you think's going to find friends more easily? There was only one way to deal with that – I had to be less boring than me and more like Jazz and Mel. Then they would like me more.

Now, sitting in the chicken shed, I do wish Stella had been there. Then none of this would have happened. And I wouldn't even be sitting here, with Mum and Dad in the house. All of us waiting to know how bad it is. They know I'm out here. They know I want to be on my own. I'm glad they're not here. I wouldn't know what to say to them. And the worst thing is, they don't even seem that cross with me.

How weird are parents?

Changing Me

I spent the week before the party in a mega state of nerves. I felt scratchy and gravelly inside, as though someone had sprinkled sand in my veins. I was probably also a grumpy cow. I'd been like that quite often recently.

Mum took me shopping and was as patient as she could be, which was really pretty patient, to be honest. I knew what I was being like, but I couldn't seem to shake it off.

I spent at least half an hour trying to choose between this black top with a red slash and this black top with a silver slash and this black top with no slash at all but a rock star's face with a sad expression. I chose none of them. And then I spent about another half-hour choosing between these murky denim jeans and a pair of those old-looking denim jeans with the faded shaded bit on the front. And even when I'd decided, I kept fretting about whether I'd chosen right.

And then there was the haircut. I tried to explain that I wanted the sides to be sort of shaggy and sloping but kind of going sideways across my face, and the back to be straight but going up a bit, and for the whole lot to look thicker than it was, but the hairdresser seemed confused. I showed her two pictures that were admittedly quite different from each other, and I said I wanted it to be partly like that one and partly like the other one, and she didn't understand that either. Mum said it was bad for my eyes to have pieces of hair covering my vision, but at least the hairdresser had the right idea there because she told my mum it was "all the rage".

I should have been more grateful to Mum. She was trying her best and I really did like the clothes, and the haircut. I had to keep my head very still when we were walking back to the car, though, or the bits at the side flew away from my face. I discovered that if I licked my finger and thumb, like Mel, I could twist the pieces into shape and they would stick there for a while. As long as I didn't turn my head or go in the wind.

When we got home I ran straight up to try all the clothes on. And my new earrings – red Ferraris. And the make-up I'd bought that day too. It was a completely different person in the mirror. It was this cool, trendy, quite unboring girl with scowling eyes and jagged hair. She wore a tight black top with tiny sleeves and a zigzag across the back. On the front was the word DUMP. In the shop, Mum had asked what DUMP meant.

"It's not meant to *mean* anything. It's just a word."

"It must mean something. Otherwise why did they put DUMP and not something completely different, like DAFFODIL or DOG or DAD? I'll ask that nice girl – she will know."

"Mum don't you *dare*! If you do that I'll..." I don't know. Do something embarrassing, as embarrassing as I could think of. But of course I wouldn't. Because then *I'd* be embarrassed.

The jeans were good. Definitely. Probably even a bit too long, but OK if I chose my shoes carefully. They were trendier than I was used to and definitely on the cool side of cool. I do KNOW what's trendy. I just can't always be bothered with it. It often means being uncomfortable. And no one in my family would particularly appreciate it. Besides, if you wore expensive designer jeans in our house you'd pretty soon sit on something nasty and then where would you be? Up the creek with an expensive dry-cleaning bill, that's where. Or, if you were really unlucky, my mum would put your designer jeans in the washing machine and

113

they'd shrink. Or come out decorated with flecks of spinach. Which actually happened once. My brothers don't like spinach and tipped their portion into the empty washing machine when my mum wasn't looking. She didn't notice when she switched it on. They said it was "a naccident".

And also, mega-trendy didn't feel like me. But that was OK – I've already said that that's the whole point: I was trying not to be me.

Anyway, so there was this girl in the mirror. And it wasn't me. I looked at her closely but it was like seeing a stranger. I took the clothes off again. And wiped off the make-up. I put my old stuff on. Now it was me. But it wasn't trendy. It wasn't Mel and Jazz's friend. It was boring.

Problem.

So, maybe I could be two me's? The Stella-comfy-home one and the new-trendy-Mel-and-Jazz one. But what would happen if Mel and Jazz came to the door when I was the wrong me?

I brushed my hair neatly and put on the new jeans and an old top. Then I messed my hair a bit. That I could deal with. Half me and half not. It was a start. I put a bit of eye-shadow back on. Yes. Kind of. I think. If I kept my eyes wide open, no one would notice.

The phone was ringing downstairs. A few moments later, Mum called me. "It's Stella!" I rushed down and grabbed the phone from her and ran back up to my room with it. "Hi, Stella!" I said as I flopped down onto my bed and lay on my stomach. And as soon as I heard her voice it all came flooding back. The Stella time. Her voice, her voice which is different from anyone else's, all balloony, as though her mouth is bigger than a usual mouth. I can always understand what Stella says, though her words are sometimes muffly, especially when she's tired. I probably haven't mentioned that before. It's not the most important thing about her. You get used to it.

I think her voice sounds like buttered toast with marshmallow melting over the edges.

(I am still totally not ever going to be a writer. I'm not trying to describe something – I'm just saying what I think.)

"Hi Becca! How are you doing?"

"Oh, you know, crazy like usual," I replied.

"And how about those girls, Mel and Jazz? You seen them again?"

"Yeah, lots. Hey and guess what, Stell! I'm having a party! It was Mel and Jazz's idea!"

"Cool! A party! So, when is it and where's my invite?"

Something like a cloud, wet and cold and grey, wrapped itself around me. Words stuck somewhere between my heart and my mouth. I couldn't speak.

I mean it was only about a few seconds or something, but it was easily long enough for me to have said, "Hey, great. Can you really come, Stell? Brill!" But I didn't. I heard the silence and Stella heard the silence.

And then we both started speaking. And then she stopped and said, "Sorry, go on," and I started rattling out the words, "Oh, I'd love you to come but I thought it'd be too difficult and your mum couldn't bring you, and you know what the trains are like for—"

"Hey, it's OK, Bec! I couldn't come anyway. I was only joking. Anyway, so tell me about Mel and Jazz. I want to know *everything*. All the goss."

I didn't want to talk about Mel and Jazz. They were part of this new time, the new me, not the Stella me. I didn't want to have to explain things. I didn't even think I could explain Jazz and Mel to Stella. There was something about them, something I wanted to be and something I almost (just every now and then) didn't like. But I needed to change myself so I did like it. I was trying to like it – the hair, the clothes, the words, the thing Mel did with her face. The hardness. How could I explain that to Stella?

"No, tell me all the school stuff first. And what's Beetroot been doing? And Creepy Crawly

Clarey? And everyone? Oh, and the javelin – how's that going?"

And before long, she had me laughing as she always did. And I wished wished WISHED I could be back in London with Stella, or Stella could come and live here too, and I never would have to bother with all the Mel and Jazz stuff.

I don't think I'm saying that because *now* I know what happened at my so-called party. But, you know, sometimes it's hard to remember what you thought at a particular moment in the past, because it gets all muddled up with what you are thinking now. Maybe I hadn't realized what my new friends were really like by then, before the party. Maybe it was only afterwards that I really wished for the Stella time. Maybe it was only when it had all gone wrong that I really thought about it properly at all.

I don't know. It's all a muddle.

If the chickens could talk, they would probably tell me the answer.

Nerves

I do remember how excited I was on the day of the party. The day of the party? What am I saying? It was only today! How can so much happen in one day? It seems like a lifetime ago.

I can feel the excitement even now. I was up too early and could hardly eat any breakfast, but of course I had to. Even the twins were excited. They kept saying they wanted to come to the party.

"No, darlings, Becca's having a party for us tomorrow. Today she's having her new friends and we are going to leave them to have a lovely time together. They are too big to want little people like you monsters getting in the way. They have important things to talk about and I'm going to take you both swimming, remember?"

"Poo," said the HP one and he pushed his specs back up his nose with a smeary finger.

"Pee," said the other one.

"Bottoms," said Mum. They giggled.

Sometimes when you're excited about something and there's a lot to do, things go wrong and everyone shouts and rushes around like – I was going to say headless chickens but I don't like that idea. But this time, nothing went wrong. We got food ready so my friends and I would only need to take it out of the fridge and down to the linny. All the sausages were cooked already, with weird dips that Dad had made the day before (with my brothers' help, but I wouldn't tell anyone that). And there was pasta salad and pizza and things on sticks. And éclairs. And sweets. And a fruit punch – lots of different fruit juices all in a huge bowl with cut-up fruit and mint leaves. And marshmallows. I sometimes wonder whether everything would have been all right if there hadn't been marshmallows.

I wanted to be able to cook the sausages on the barbecue during the party but obviously that wasn't allowed. I did have a bit of an argument about that but I knew I wasn't going to get very far. Parents have this big fear of fire. I hoped Mel wasn't expecting to be able to use the barbecue. I almost wished Dad hadn't finished building it. Mind you, it probably wouldn't have made any difference in the end. You don't need a barbecue to make a fire, after all.

Dad had a migraine by the time we had finished all this, but that didn't matter because he could just lie in bed instead of working at his desk. He'd still be out of the way, maybe even more so. I realize now that that sounds selfish, but I wasn't thinking about anything except the fact that I had told Mel and Jazz my parents would be out. And that made me sound definitely cool and not boring.

The plan was that my mum and brothers would leave the house at about twelve and Dad would hide himself away in his bed. My friends would come at about one and we would just hang out and do whatever and eat when we wanted and just, I suppose, chill and do stuff and... I don't know. What are you supposed to do at parties? I'd never thought about it before. You just ... have fun. You don't think about it. I was thinking about it. A lot.

What if no one said anything? What if they thought I was boring? What if they all had a totally awful time and thought I was the most uncool person they had ever met? I felt sick. My stomach kept doing this shrinking thing like a balloon that's going down and it's all crinkly and disgusting to touch.

I took loads of things down to the linny and tidied it all up during the morning. I let my brothers help me. They were actually quite helpful and they didn't go anywhere near the stream. Personally, I thought Mum and Dad were being paranoid forbidding the twins to go near it. I thought it looked so shallow that no one could come to any harm. I mean, in most places it was only just up to my brothers' knees.

Anyway, the twins liked being asked to help and they grinned huge grins, as though it was their own birthday. When I told the not-HP one to stop picking his nose while he was counting cups out, he grinned some more and said, "Sorry, MacLorry," but he did actually stop straightaway. They helped me carry two small tables and we covered them with cloths so you wouldn't know they were plastic children's tables.

Then the HP twin did an amazing thing. He picked flowers – only daisies, but he got an eggcup and put the daisies in with some water. They were a bit droopy because he hadn't snapped the stems very well, more of a sort of squashing tug, and they were all different lengths. But my four-year-old brother had picked flowers for my party!

I got changed before my family went out. When I went downstairs, Dad was in the kitchen getting some ice to put on his neck. He saw me coming carefully down the stairs in my too-long jeans, grinned through his heavy eyes and said that if I would come into the kitchen and walk about a bit from side to side we wouldn't have to clean the kitchen floor.

"Da-ad!" I said. "Just because the last time you were in fashion it was like a hundred years ago!"

"Yeah, man, I'm just an old hippy – I mean *like* whadoo I know?" he said, trying to do an impression of a cool person but not quite getting it right. Even through his migraine, he could still smile.

I grinned. I did. I felt like grinning then. Yes, nervous, but good nervous at that point. I think it was the last time I grinned.

"Like the earrings, Becca," said Mum. Mum always likes my earrings. Your mum liking your earrings is not exactly the point.

Anyway, Mum and the boys left, and Dad took his ice pack and went up to bed. I was on my own. I put on some make-up. My hand was wobbly so the eye-liner went too thick and smudged. I rubbed it off and tried again. I looked like a sick panda. Mascara was easier, until I poked myself in the eye and it went all watery so everything ran together and I had to start again. Lip-gloss. I had to remember not to close my lips properly.

I went to the linny and fiddled around with drinks and chairs and stuff. Then I unfiddled the chairs and stacked them behind the straw – I didn't think we wanted chairs. Too much like a school event. There was nothing else to do. My

CD player was there, with an extension lead plugging it into the socket in the linny. And all my CDs in a box. Cushions.

Fifteen minutes to go. A churning feeling in my stomach now. I went to see the chickens. They didn't know anything was going on.

The summer sun buzzed with heat. Cocky the cockerel stood in the shade of a bushy tree. The chickens pecked around him.

I checked their water. Full. I checked their grit. Fine. I scattered a bit of grain. They pecked at it.

I went into the shed. That lovely syrupy chickeny rumble. There was Stella. Sitting on her nest, one eye closed.

"Hi, Stella," I said. She opened the other eye. She looked at me with her head on one side, as if to say, "Yes?"

"I wish I were a chicken," I said. "No worries about anything. No parties to get nervous about. No new friends to impress."

"Oh yeah? You think we have it so easy? What about foxes? And that Cocky bossing us around and pecking us. And have you ever *thought* about how painful it is laying an egg that's bigger than your own foot? And then there's lice, and cold weather and – eugh! – rain, when the grain turns to mush and your feet get soggy and your feathers go heavy and the shed stinks of wet chicken and—"

"Yeah, OK, Stella, I get the message. We all have our problems, don't we?"

It's OK, I haven't finally lost it. Chickens don't talk and Stella was no different from any other chicken in that way. But you could just imagine that's what she would say. And the real Stella would also say, "Look outside yourself, Becca. There's a world out there and it's a brilliant world." And I'd smile and the smile would become a grin and suddenly the world WOULD seem a brilliant place and nothing else would matter.

I heard tyres, a horn hooting. They were here! My stomach span in a circle – I'll swear it did. I ran out of the chicken shed without even saying goodbye to Stella and shut the gate after me. I know I shut the gate.

I have to have a pause before I start to say what happened at the party. Looking back on it, there are so many things that could have gone wrong, it's amazing they all didn't.

Once, in primary school, we did this thing about safety. We had to look at a picture and circle all the things that could be dangerous. If there was a picture of my party, you'd definitely want to put a circle round the stream and the barbecue. And me leaving the chicken gate open. (Well, obviously I did, I realize that now. I must have done.) Then

Mel's brother and his chicken-eating snake called Saddam. And the alcohol that Mel would have with her. Me with diabetes, and worrying instead of eating. The only adult asleep in his bed.

But the main thing, which you wouldn't be able to show in a picture, is the fact that anyone with half a brain can tell that Mel and Jazz care a million times more about themselves than they do about anyone else. Seems obvious now.

And that is why I am sitting here in the chicken shed, and it's growing dark outside, and I can't face going back to the house just now.

So, as I said, I'm going to have a pause. I'm going to take a deep breath. And...

Party Time

Even now it's hard to explain. It seems quite confusing and, to be honest, I can't remember all of it. I suppose that's not surprising, is it? They say that at times of stress your brain goes all shattery and only picks up some things and shuts the others out. And I was having a hypo for part of it, so that makes everything confused.

So, what do I remember?

Everyone arriving. The car driven by Mel's brother. Not a car, one of those open-backed trucks, with Mel and Jazz and another girl who turned out to be Sophie sitting in the cab and three boys and two girls wedged in the open bit at the back, shrieking and yelling as they rolled up our drive. One of the boys stood up too soon and fell over. He swore and they all laughed. It wasn't that funny.

Their voices loud. The boys roaring. The girls

squealing stupidly. Mel's brother getting out of the driver's seat, his long spindly legs unfolding like a daddy-long-legs'.

I remember what Mel and Jazz were wearing. All black. Just black, black, black. As they came closer, I felt small and silly and boring already. I felt like a lump. Not tall and skinny and like something out of a magazine.

My Ferrari earrings were nowhere near going to make enough difference.

Mel's top had this weird symbol on the front. A sort of circle with a cross sticking out of the side of it and some letters in Gothic writing. Her eyes were thick with black make-up. Her arms were heavy with silver bangles and a black leather thing wrapped round above her elbow. Jazz's trousers kind of hung off her hips and her top was so short you could see her stomach. And in her belly button was something shiny and she even had a tattoo thing drawn above it. They both had black nail varnish.

I had forgotten about nail varnish. I was furious with myself. How could I have forgotten? I had even bought some specially.

I think that was when I realized. When I came to my senses. Really realized and had to admit to myself: they were not my type. It wasn't any one thing – not the tattoo, the black, anything. Those things were OK, no big deal – not my scene but no big deal. It was just the whole thing, the whole image. The kind of atmosphere that flowed off them. It wasn't me. I could never be like them and actually, really, I didn't even want to be like them. I was out of my league. And it wasn't even a league I wanted to be in. I had made a huge mistake. And now I just wanted the afternoon to be over.

They all walked towards me. This crowd of loud and laughing kids, all grinning at me. And Mel's brother. The one who was chucked out of school for something to do with alcohol. What was he doing here? Why was he walking towards me as well? He wasn't coming to my party, was he? He was eighteen – what would he want with a twelve-year-old's party?

"Hiya Becksie," shrieked Mel. "This is Sophe an' Joe an' Paulo an' Sassy an' Sharky an' Corally. Dee couldn't make it. Oh an' this is my big bro, Mark."

"Hi everyone," I said. "Thanks for coming." How boring did I sound? Like a parent or something.

Was Mark going to go or not?

"Everything's in the linny."

The three girls I hadn't met, and still didn't know which was which, did this kind of looking at each other thing with rolling eyes and hands on hips. Then, as though it was rehearsed, they put their left hands in the air, snapped their fingers twice and all hit the palms together in the middle. And fell around laughing. I don't know what it was about. It wasn't easy to laugh at, but I did my best to join in. The three boys, on the other hand, did this thing where they put their hands upside down under their chins and dangled the fingers, wiggling them, and they said, in this sort of whiny high voice, "Woooooooo, linny!"

"Shut up, it's just a word for barn. Don't you even know that?" grinned Mel.

But I still felt uncomfortable. If I had been arriving at a stranger's house for a party, I'd have walked up the path all polite and smiling and a bit shy, and introduced myself and waited for the person whose house it was to invite me in. This lot just ran up the drive with Jazz leading the way towards the side of the house where the path to the linny was.

So that just left me with Mel and her brother.

He was about the scariest person I had seen, apart from on the Tube in London. But then I wouldn't have had to talk to him or even look at him. His clothes were disgusting – black, dirty and torn, and obviously smelly.

He had a leather strap wrapped round one arm,

a black tattoo on his other arm, and his eyebrow was pierced with something that looked like a torpedo. His hair looked as though it hadn't been washed for a month. Wet red spots covered his forehead and there was one huge one above his lip.

He probably thought he was just so cool.

"Yeah, well, better be going," he said. Thank goodness for that, I thought. He was looking at me in a way I seriously did not like.

"Oh, show Becks Saddam first, Mar. Go on, you said you would." Mel turned to me. "Saddam's got to go to the vet – some sort of fungus." She shrieked for the others to come back. "Hey, you lot, wait for us." They stopped and waited in the distance. Next to the chicken run.

I had absolutely zero desire to see this snake, but what could I say? Mark grudgingly lifted a large bag out of the truck. He carried it carefully and put it on the ground. It looked heavy. And it moved. He undid the drawstring at the top of the bag and slowly pulled out an enormous snake with black and grey and brown bits. It began to coil itself around his arm. I watched in horror, frozen to the spot. I have never thought about snakes that much, since I never expected to meet one, but my heart was clattering like gunfire and I really wished I was not meeting one right now.

"Go on, you can touch him," said Mel. "He won't bite."

"No, it's OK," I said.

"Go on, stupid, he feels nice. Look," and Mel stroked the snake. She pouted her lips into a kiss just a little way from its face. Saddam looked around at her slowly and stared, but did nothing. I had to touch it. Anything to get rid of Mark and his horrible reptile as soon as possible. I moved my hand towards...

That was when I heard a shriek from the others. I looked round. And *that* was when I saw that the chickens had escaped. Saddam's eyes flickered towards them. His tongue slipped out and I swear he licked his lips.

I ran. The chickens were strutting about near the gate of the chicken run. The open gate. The girls were laughing and trying to catch them, but you can't catch a chicken while you're shrieking. One of the boys dived at a chicken and almost caught it. Another boy dived and did catch it. But as soon as he had it in his arms he let it go and it ran squawking away.

Please Dad, don't look out of your window! Actually, I don't think he'd have seen from that angle, but the last thing I wanted was him coming down when the others all thought there were no adults about.

"OK, everyone go up to the lin— barn. I'll deal with this." No one went. They all just stood around laughing. I grabbed a chicken from behind and gently put her through the gate and shut it. Cocky was sitting on a stump crowing furiously, which was no help at all.

I didn't look back to see what Mark was doing but I hoped he would get the message and take his horrible snake away.

The next bit is confusion. Catching chickens, putting them safely in the chicken run. Someone trying to herd a chicken towards the gate, opening it, another chicken running out again. Girls shrieking with a mixture of laughter and pointless shrieking. Mel's voice. Mark's voice. That snake wrapped around his arm. The snake slithering onto the ground. Moving towards the chickens. Panic! No!

The chickens seeing the snake. Squawking. Cocky seeing the snake. Crowing. Cocky running towards the closed gate. Leaping onto the fence post. Leaping off and running towards Saddam with his beak outstretched. My heart crashing. Feeling dizzy panic. The chickens running towards the gate. Me opening it. The chickens running through. Me closing it.

Cocky standing there in front of Saddam, his wings outstretched. Saddam staring, tensed, ready to strike. Me stuck, not able to move. Squealing from the girls. Why wouldn't they SHUT UP? Dad! I need you! I don't care about the party any more.

Mark calmly picking Saddam up and beginning to slither him back into his bag.

Everything coming back into focus.

The chickens were safe. Cocky simply crowed one more time, a huge long crow, as though to say, "See how brave I am? The bravest cockerel in the West, me!" And he snapped his beak towards Saddam's disappearing head, turned and leapt onto the fence post again, before jumping down among the chickens and herding them noisily into the shed.

Mark was grinning, a sort of greasy sneery grin, like Mel's but with spottier skin. "You din't need to worry. 'E ate a whole rabbit this morning. Won't eat till next week now. Anyway, must be going. Got to see a man about a snake." And off he went, lolling on his long legs and spitting on our drive.

No one seemed upset by all this. They seemed to think it was hilarious. I was still feeling a little dizzy. Sudden exercise is something you have to be careful about with diabetes – it's fine as long as you eat properly, but I hadn't. I brushed the feeling aside and concentrated on getting everyone up to the linny.

Even though the panic had gone, I felt a definite sense of wanting this day to be over. A certain fear. A strange and panicky feeling that this was not really my party at all and that I had absolutely no control over what was going to happen.

Then what I remember is this:

Everyone seeming to think the linny was brilliant. People taking off their shoes and some of them wading in the stream and splashing a bit. The sun burning down. Jazz and Sophie and Paulo coming with me to the kitchen to get the food and drink. Me quickly snatching a piece of pizza and eating it. Me being a bit scared of Paulo because he was cool and had taken a lot of trouble over gelling his hair, and quite liking Sophie, even though she was supposed to be a tart. Paulo picking up a sausage and two marshmallows and laughing, and then eating them all in one mouthful and never looking at me.

Me telling myself that perhaps it would be all right. Trying to calm myself. Trying to smile and grin and laugh and squeal along with the others. Not wanting to. Looking at my watch every few minutes but the hands never moving.

Fiddling with my Ferrari earrings so much that a wheel came off.

Going back to the linny. Finding that Mel and the others were lighting a fire under the barbecue.

One girl – Sassy? – playing with a lighter, just flicking it over and over, as though she'd never seen a flame before. Mel saying, "I just *love* toasted marshmallows, Becks!" Mel sticking a marshmallow on a fork and holding it in the fire. Not knowing what to say. Not saying anything but just moving all the dried sticks and anything else that might burn away from it. Standing, watching, trying to take in everything with my eyes, everything that might go wrong.

Not knowing everyone's names and having to work it out gradually and try to remember. Feeling invisible.

Everyone taking their phones out of their pockets or bags and laying them out carefully on the table. Like some kind of film where all the cowboys lay their guns down before a card game.

Spreading the food and drinks out on the tables, offering it round, feeling like an old mother hen. People grabbing. Not knowing whether they actually liked it or not because pretty much no one said thank you or anything. Feeling boring. Feeling as though someone had tied a piece of string round my tongue and no words would come. Feeling that each time I did say something my voice was different from everyone else's – silly, Londony, babyish, dull, stuck-up... I don't know, just that it jarred like grit in an ice cream. Not being able to join in their conversation because they talked about so much stuff and names I'd never heard of that it might as well have been a foreign language. Feeling like a stranger at my own party.

Mel suddenly saying, "OK, let's make this party swing, guys." And her taking a bottle of lemonade out of her bag. Didn't she like the fruit punch? Mel tipping the contents of the bottle into the punch. And me realizing that it wasn't lemonade. The dizzy feeling getting worse.

Quickly having something to eat again. Marshmallows. Four of them all at once.

Mel ladling the new fruit punch into everyone's cups.

Me knowing that I did NOT want to drink this. With diabetes, alcohol is another thing you have to be careful about. I'd never had any, except a bit of cider at Christmas and stuff, and I didn't know what this probably-vodka would do. Even without diabetes, I didn't want it.

Me not being able to say no. Taking my cup and pretending to sip at it. Spilling it accidentally on purpose but Mel filling it up again. Me not drinking it. Well, one sip, but not enough to make any difference. Me saying, "Mmmm, nice." The boys drinking quickly. Mel too. Paulo and a boy I think was Sharky, but might have been Joe, starting to hit each other but laughing at the same time.

Mel turning to Jazz and saying in a loud, stupid pretend-drunk voice, like the sort you hear on television, "'K everyone, le's play truth or dare."

But not having time to worry because suddenly a voice. Mum, calling me. Looking at my watch. The party had only been going less than an hour. Mum had promised to be away at least two and a half hours and then NOT come to the linny but stay out of the way. She had promised! A horrible panicky anger. This was not how my party was meant to be, with me worrying about everything and everything being totally outside my control.

Me saying, "Back in a sec," to the others and hurrying away towards the house. Taking my drink with me and tipping it into a bush.

"Mum, what are you doing here?"

"I'm so sorry, Becca darling. I didn't want to come and disturb you. Small problem. Case of a small boy and a cut lip." Me looking towards the car. The HP twin sitting in the back with the door open and something bloody pressed to his lip, his eyes staring out from above it. Him whimpering a bit. Mum continuing, "I phoned the surgery and I can take him there now and they'll look at it and maybe stitch it. I'll probably only be less than an hour but I just thought I'd drop Beech here…"

That's it, I've said it. Don't suppose it matters now, does it?

Beech, as in the tree, because in those days, when Beech was born, they had this thing about trees. They used to hug a tree every morning to "commune with the spirit of the tree". You're probably not that surprised now. And I don't care any more anyway.

Me saying, "Oh Mum, can't Dad look after him?" And Mum looking quite unusually cross and stressed. "Look, darling, I know it's your party but Dad is really not feeling well and it's such a short time. Beech can get some colouring stuff or puzzles and he can sit in the linny and he'll be no trouble. Please, Becca, don't be difficult." And Mum looking so small and upset and harassed that I had to say it was fine, even though it wasn't.

I mean, how uncool is it to have your four-year-old brother hanging around at your twelfth birthday party?

And me taking Beech to get some things to occupy him and saying to him in a horribly foul and nasty voice, which I now regret, "If you even speak one word to my friends or do anything to irritate me, you horrible little boy, we'll roast you on the barbecue." And him looking shocked and frightened, and saying nothing but giving an odd little sob as though he'd been crying a lot earlier and it was still stuck inside him. And me roughly wiping his nose so that my friends wouldn't see that my brother was snotty. And leading him towards the linny, walking so fast that he had to keep doing a little skip to keep up.

The girls looking half horrified but half giggling and one of the boys saying in a silly loud slurry voice, "Look, it's dinner. Get that barby going, Mel." And me saying, "Sorry, guys, bad news. It's my brother. The other one's had to go to the doctor. Don't worry, he won't get in the way."

Rolling eyeballs and sulky faces.

Jazz saying, "Come on, Becca, come over here." Me giving Beech a furious look, which he perfectly well understood. The boys calling Beech to play football with them. Near the stream, but that was OK because the boys were with him. And it was just shallow there anyway.

Sitting down in a circle with the girls. A growing breeze making the fire crackle and flame. The paper napkins fluttering.

"'K, birthday girl goes first. Truth or dare, Becks?" asks the one who I think is called Corally. Blonde, thin, keeps putting on more lip-gloss. Smooth orange face.

"Truth." Definitely not feeling daring.

"Do you fancy Sharky?"

Easy. Even if I'm not quite sure which one he is. "No."

"Why?" asks Mel crossly. "What's wrong with him?"

Oh God, Mel is going out with Sharky, isn't she? Well, wouldn't it have been worse if I'd said yes?

Someone saying, "Shut up, Mel – you can't ask two questions."

"My turn," says the one who I think is Sassy. Brown messy hair. Too fat for her tight low-waist jeans. Sorry, but she was. "Dare!" she squeals.

Silence. Sophie prodding me hard on the shoulder and saying, "You have to think of the dare, Becca. Hurry up!"

Growing dizziness. Black-like rainy stuff. Needing to eat something. Concentrate.

Not being able to think of anything. Come on, think of something!

"Come on! Hurry up! Can't you think of anything?"

Me saying at last, "Eat a piece of pizza with marshmallow on top."

Sassy saying, "That's stupid! That's not even daring!" and stuffing some pizza and marshmallow into her mouth. The breeze blowing her hair into her food. Her pulling a strand of hair out of her mouth and it being all sticky with marshmallow and pizza.

Needing to tell someone about feeling dizzy.

Beech knows what to do. But Beech is playing football with the boys. He can't see me. Can't see what's happening.

Dimly aware of the game continuing. Me grinning and trying to laugh at the same time as everyone else. Mel choosing a dare and being told to drink a cup of punch without stopping. Everyone shrieking. Her standing up and doing it, and then pretending to fall over.

A spark exploding from the fire and landing on someone's arm. Sophie. More shrieking. Sophie pretending to be seriously injured and doing a fake faint backwards onto the ground and spilling someone's drink. Everyone grabbing their phones away from the drink.

Me standing up, falling over. Voices, tumbling. Tongue funny. Spinning away into the rushing sound. Water. Head swimming. Sweet water in my head. No, sweetness in my mouth. Eat this, Becca. Beech. Beech. His face above mine. Falling into focus. The water rushing away. Chocolate in my mouth.

Sitting up. Everyone's faces around me. Embarrassed. "Sorry, just fainted. Must be the heat," I say.

"She's got dying beetles," Beech is saying proudly. That's what he always calls it. We think it's so funny, we don't correct him.

141

Puzzled faces. "Diabetes." My voice still sounding odd. Needing to go and tell Dad. Still frightened. By the hypo and the heat and the way the party is sliding out of control. The way the boys are kicking the ball so hard and suddenly noticing that Beech is drinking from a beaker – how did that happen? And snatching it from him just in time and then noticing that some paper napkins have blown into the fire and the flames were...

Shouting! Everyone shouting. Rushing to the stream to fill shoes, beakers, anything, with water. And Beech, Beech helping, and helping brilliantly, rushing to and fro with a tiny beaker of water, and being the last one to go to the stream because he hadn't noticed that the fire was out. Then Beech dropping his beaker into the stream and the beaker floating away quickly towards the deeper bit and Beech suddenly not being there – now over there, far away by the deep black bit, leaning over the bank and slipping and screaming. Me seeing this in slow motion – and Mel, who was nearest, shouting, "Quick, Becca, quick, your brother!" and all of us rushing but Mel getting there first and jumping in and grabbing him before his frightened face could be swept away. Mel standing there waist-deep and holding my brother under the arms and pulling him to the side.

Mel, who by then I had begun to hate with a deep, gut-wrenching fury, with a tongue-tingling disgust, with something that rushed through my whole body like fire, Mel saving my brother from the water.

Wide, wide, white frightened faces. Hands grabbing him and pulling him and Mel out.

Beech crying and ashen-faced and clinging to Mel and then holding out his hands to me. And Mel with blood pouring from a cut on her foot and all of us rushing up to the house and me shouting for Dad and Mel hopping with one hand on Sharky's shoulder. Dad asking what happened and us all trying to tell him at the same time. But it not mattering because Beech was all right and Dad was there and I didn't care about whether anyone thought I was boring or not. Dad looking at Mel's foot and deciding she didn't need to go to hospital. And no one saying anything much as he cleaned and bandaged her foot. And me going to get her some dry clothes.

And I know that it was then, as I came downstairs with some jeans and passed the open front door, just when I was starting to panic at the thought of how it had so nearly been much worse, that I suddenly smelt it. Smoke. Carried on the breeze.

*　　*　　*

And that, that is the whole story of why I am now sitting in the chicken shed alone, while the firefighters put out the fire in the linny. The fire that must have started because we mustn't have put it out completely and the breeze must have blown a piece of burning napkin onto the straw bales. The linny is burning down and everything is ruined.

And that is why, now that I've told it all, I really do know whose fault it was. All of it. Mine. For thinking that when you want friends, you have to change to get them. For not caring about the right things and caring too much about the total rubbish.

Now

I can hear a car. Voices. I hear the gate open and footsteps are scrunching on the ground outside. Someone is coming. The door opens.

It's Jazz. I shine my torch in her face. Her face is streaked and red and ugly. Good. "Oh yeah, Jazz? The pretty one?" Not any more.

"Can I come in?" she says. I don't particularly want her here. I don't know what to say to her.

"What are you doing here?" I ask, my voice strong and angry. Surprising myself.

"I came to say sorry."

She sniffs. She is crying again. I move the torch away from her face.

"My mum brought me. She's in your house. She's furious with me. She always told me Mel was trouble. But it wasn't just Mel. It was me. I knew what we were doing was wrong, at your party, the alcohol and stuff. We messed up your party."

I am silent.

"I feel lousy," she says.

"Yeah, well." Big deal.

"I'm sorry, really sorry."

Silence. And now I have to say what I really think. There's no point in pretending any more. Even to myself. And so I speak.

"It was all my fault anyway. I was so trying to impress everyone." My voice is breaking up and quivery. I don't care. I continue, pushing the words out, however cracked they sound. "I tried to be like you and Mel, but I'm not like you and Mel, and I don't even want to be, if you must know. But I wanted you to think I was cool and all that stuff. I just went along with everything. I didn't have to. I just did, so it's all my fault."

"Well, whatever, but we were total prats. You must have hated us."

"Yeah, probably did, if I think about it."

"You know about the diabetes?"

"What?"

"Why didn't you tell us?"

"I don't know. I just didn't want to. It's a hassle explaining it and everyone always wants to ask questions and stuff."

There is a silence. Then she speaks again, a different voice, small. "I like the noise the chickens make. Do they have names?"

"See that one looking at you through one eye?"

She looks. "The white one?"

"She's called Stella."

"Like your friend."

"Yes."

"Can I ask you a question? About Stella?"

"I know what you want to ask. You want to know why she is in a wheelchair."

"Yeah. Is it OK to ask that?" She is trying. She really is. Amazing how she seems almost frightened of me, eager to please me. As if she is really thinking about what I feel. How things change.

"Stella was in a car accident. Drunk driver. Two years ago. Her head was injured and she had to have an operation. It made her muscles on one side weak. Her face too. It makes her voice different. But she's getting better and she can walk a bit with crutches. And she's going to do the javelin at sports day. I bet she wins."

"She looked nice. In the photo."

"She is nice. She thinks about other people."

Jazz knows what I am saying. She pauses. Then, "I'm sorry."

I believe her now. I might even give her another chance. Might. Stella the chicken looks over to me. She blinks at me. "Good decision," Stella says approvingly.

"How's your brother?" asks Jazz.

"Beech? He's fine. Just got a fright. He won't be going near the stream again."

"Beech? Is that his name? As in the sandy thing by the sea?"

"No. As in the tree." I don't care any more.

"Oh. Right. The tree." She looks at me uncertainly. "Well, I suppose a girl could be called Hazel. And we once had a dog called Willow."

"Yeah, and we had a girl at school called Cherry." I grinned.

"What about your other brother? What's he called? Oak? Chestnut?"

"Larch."

"Larch. Oh. Right." She turns away. She is trying not to laugh. I can tell by how stiff her shoulders are. I want to laugh myself.

"Yeah, Larch. As in the tree."

"Your family are... I don't know..."

"Barking?" I say.

"Yeah," she agrees, laughing. And then laughing louder as she suddenly gets the joke.

And it's almost, sort of, nearly, just a bit, like being with Stella again. Not minding. Not hiding.

Voices are coming, footsteps. Dad calling. I run outside the chicken shed. Jazz follows. The chickens chirrup. Cocky looks up, puzzled by this night-time activity. Dad and Jazz's mother are there. Jazz goes to her mother. Dad is coming towards me.

A fire engine goes past, away from the linny and towards the road. The firefighters are waving, their faces tired and black.

"Dad, I'm really sorry," I say, "about everything." Tears start to prickle.

"It wasn't your fault," says Dad.

"It was. It was totally my fault."

He smiles, tired. His migraine will be fading now. It always does in the evening. "Actually, it really wasn't. The firefighters said it started at the electric point – the socket was old and dangerous. We should have had it checked, I suppose. Anyway, I'm afraid your stereo is a goner. And the linny will have to be repaired – maybe knocked down first. But, don't worry – the insurance will cover it. The fire really wasn't your fault, Becca. And the other stuff, well, we'll talk about it later, but I guess you probably know everything I'm going to say? I guess you could probably say it yourself." He puts his arms round my shoulders and we walk back to the house.

The relief is huge, enormous, like a hot-air balloon floating away on the wind. Like the sun coming out from behind the biggest cloud. Egg-yellow, banana-bright.

I know there are lots of things that were my

fault. Even if the fire wasn't. But I know what they are and Dad knows I know what they are. He knows that next time I'll do it differently. I know next time I'll just be myself.

The One With the...

Mel and Jazz came round the next day, just as we were finishing lunch. It was my birthday, though it didn't feel like a birthday. I had spent the morning helping clear up the burnt stuff from the linny and I was just about to go out again when I heard the doorbell. And there they were. I didn't want to see Mel. She made me feel a mixture of anger and shame. She ruined my party. She saved my brother.

I was in scruffy jeans, filthy from picking up sooty things, smears of black on my face. Clean hands but that was all. No earrings.

"Hi, Becca," said Jazz.

"Hi," I said.

"Happy birthday," said Jazz. Mel muttered the same.

They looked at each other. Kind of a bit embarrassed? Maybe.

"Can we come in?" asked Jazz. Mel chewed a bit of skin on her finger.

Mum and Dad came out of the kitchen then. They looked quite normal standing there. Nothing embarrassing that I could see. No bits of inventions sticking out from behind Mum's ears. Dad was wearing proper shoes. My brothers stood there, just staring. They didn't even have food spilt on them. They didn't pick their noses, or do that being-sick thing or suddenly fall over for no reason at all. They didn't say "dog poo".

Jazz spoke first, "We want to say that we are really sorry about yesterday." She nudged Mel.

"And we've come to help," mumbled Mel. "Clear up or something."

"Thank you, girls," said Mum. "I think that's a very good idea. How's your foot, Jel?"

"Mel, Mum," I said.

"Yes, of course, Mel. How's your foot?"

"OK," muttered Mel. She was doing a lot of muttering.

"I know I said this yesterday, Mel," said Dad. "But thank you again for what you did with Beech. I've already finished that fence – should have done it before."

She didn't even smile then. She looked as though the last place in the world she wanted to be was here.

"Right ho, shall we get to work?" said Mum.

We walked up to the linny, not talking but listening to Dad giving them the lecture which I had already had. You can imagine everything he said. I thought he was wasting his time and normally I'd have been totally embarrassed listening to him telling off friends of mine, but I didn't care about that any more. And they deserved it. The twins walked as far from Mel and Jazz as they could. Mum walked in front. She walked straight past her invention shed without even veering towards it.

I could feel my new phone, my birthday present, inside my back pocket. I would leave it there. I didn't need to show Jazz and Mel. Only Stella and my real friends could have my number.

Jazz nudged Mel and Mel handed me an envelope from her bag. She still wouldn't look at me. I opened it as we walked along.

In it was a card. On the front, it said "Sorry" in big decorated letters, with other small pictures like party hats, candles, chickens, pizza and a whole load of other things that reminded me much too much of yesterday. And at the bottom it said, "Oh, and PS – Happy Birthday!" It was quite artistic, actually. Not brilliant but not bad. You could tell they had tried. But they would definitely never be artists when they grew up, though, not weird or normal ones.

I opened the card. Inside was a drawing of a girl. The face didn't look much like me, though the hair was right. And she was wearing the clothes I'd been wearing yesterday. But you could tell this girl was me because she had the hugest earrings in the shape of a catwalk model. And she had other earrings in her hands – the Marilyn Monroe handbag ones, the New York Apple ones, the crocodile-eating-its-tail ones, the Manolo Blahnik ones and the red Ferrari ones. And underneath, it said: "To Becca, the girl with the COOLEST earrings ever!"

Heaven is moments like that. You just melt. You melt from the stomach upwards and the feeling sweeps right through you like warm water between your toes.

Who knows if I'll ever be proper friends with them? The only thing I do know is that next time it won't be me who's changing. I never needed to change in the first place. I already was who I wanted to be.

"Oh yes – Becca? She's the one with the coolest earrings ever."

THE OUTCASTS OF
19 SCHUYLER PLACE
E.L. KONIGSBURG

The summer is just beginning, and Margaret is having a miserable time at camp – her cabin-mates, the Meadowlarks, are picking on her. So she's delighted when her beloved, eccentric uncles and their dog, Tartufo, whisk her back to their home at 19 Schuyler Place.

But Margaret soon learns that her uncles are in need of rescuing too. The three giant towers they have spent the last forty-five years building in their backyard are under threat by the city council. To Margaret, the towers are irreplaceable works of art. They sing of joy, integrity and history ... and Margaret is determined to make sure they always will.

From the incomparable E.L. Konigsburg, twice winner of the prestigious Newbery Medal, comes this rousing story about art and the fierce preservation of individuality.

THE STARTHORN TREE
KATE FORSYTH

Under winter's cold shroud, the son of light lies
Though the summer sun burns high in the skies.
With the last petal of the starthorn tree
His wandering spirit shall at last slip free…

The young Count of Estelliana lies mysteriously ill
and his people suffer under the rule of the cruel
regent Lord Zavion. Then Durrik, a local peasant
boy, has a vision about the fate of the Count, and
he and his best friend Pedrin are catapulted into
the adventure of their lives.

Following the strange riddle of Durrik's dream,
the pair set out on a quest to find a cure for their
leader and a way to free their people. But not only
must they put up with some extraordinary travel-
ling companions, the children must also survive
the hazards of the Perilous Forest and all that lies
in wait for them there…